HOLY SHIFT

New Orleans Nocturnes
Book Eight

CARRIE PULKINEN

Holy Shift

ISBN: 978-1-957253-37-4

He's got the right fluff.
She's living on a prayer.
They'll both need more bounce to the ounce if
they're going to save Easter this year.

Earthbound angel Destiny Monroe has three weeks to perform a miracle or she'll lose her wings and her immortality. That should be no big deal. She is an angel, after all.

The problem?

It takes months and cutting through miles of red tape to get a miracle approved by the higher-ups. More months than Destiny has left.

She might as well kiss her wings goodbye.

But when she falls head over halo for Pete Hasen, the smoking hot rabbit shifter who's also an immortal fae, she's determined to get her miracle approved so she can spend eternity with him.

The next problem?

Pete happens to be the Easter Bunny, and Destiny might have accidentally given him amnesia.

Whoops.

It will take a miracle for Pete to get his memory back in time to save Easter. Lucky for him, the angel of his dreams might just make that happen...

CHAPTER

ONE

"Demon farts don't even stink anymore, thanks to me. Isn't that miracle enough?" Destiny Monroe cleared the nervous muck from her throat and wiped her palms on her pristine white gown.

She glanced at her lap and tried not to cringe.

You'd think the magic that morphed her clothes into this standard issue angel uniform the moment she crossed into Divine Grace, Inc. would've cleaned her hands too—perfection was a must in the angelic realm—but no. A smear of pale blue frosting from the baby shower cake she'd been decorating stretched from her hip to the middle of her thigh.

Gabriela folded her arms on the golden desk between them and made a *tsk* sound. "You should have washed your hands before you answered my summons."

Another bit of frosting lingered on Destiny's thumb, so she stuck it in her mouth, swiping it with her tongue before folding her hands in her lap to cover the stain.

"The message felt urgent." She tried to hold the archangel's gaze, but the intensity in Gabriela's silver eyes forced her to look away.

The expansive office had alabaster walls, a polished white marble floor, and a bookcase filled from top to bottom with golden "Seraph of the Month" trophies and plaques. Behind the desk, a massive floor-to-ceiling window provided a view of the repository below, where dozens upon dozens of lower-level angels rushed about, reshelving books, filing paperwork, and smiling while they worked themselves to... Well, not to death. Angels didn't die, but Destiny was sure as sugar she'd want to after working down there for a decade or so.

Divine Grace, Inc. was the governing body that managed all the angels in all the realms. Michelle was the big boss, of course, and she handed down all the rules from the higher ups. Her gaggle of archangels acted as middle management, doling out orders and making sure the almighty angel of angels' laws were followed to the letter.

Because heaven forbid the egotistical dictator lift a wing and do the work herself.

Destiny sighed and closed her eyes for a long blink. That wasn't very angel-like of her to think, but what could they expect? Gabriela kept winning those ridiculous awards because she kissed Michelle's tush every chance she got. She also kept the angels in her dominion under a heavy thumb.

Everything ran smoothly. Mistakes were not allowed.

And now Destiny sat in this cushiony chair with its obscene amount of fluff, trying not to squirm as her boss reprimanded her...not for screwing up. No, Destiny wasn't in the hot seat for anything she'd done. Not this time, anyway. It was what she *hadn't* done that had landed her here, under Gabriela's reproachful gaze.

"How long has it been since you've graced this realm?" the archangel asked.

Destiny straightened her spine, drawing her feathered wings closer to her back. "I don't know. A while."

"One hundred and fifty-two years." Gabriela

leaned back, resting her elbows on the arms of the chair and steepling her fingers.

Destiny clenched her jaw, fighting the urge to tell her she shouldn't ask questions to which she already knew the answers.

"How long has it been since you've performed an actual, office-sanctioned miracle on Earth? And do not mention demon flatulence in my presence again. You're lucky your 'cure' for that so-called ailment was a mere side effect of your angel food cake recipe. Applying for approval after a miracle has been performed is forbidden, which I am certain you know."

"I…" Demon farts were more than a *so-called ailment*. They were a gosh dang epidemic, and all of New Orleans was breathing easier now, thanks to her. She pressed her lips into a line and waited for Gabriela to answer her own question.

"It's been one hundred and two years since you've performed a miracle, Destiny." She arched a judgmental brow. "At minimum, how often must an earthbound angel perform an office-sanctioned miracle if she wishes to remain in that realm?"

Destiny's throat thickened as she waited for the archangel to answer for her. When she didn't, she forced out a response, "At least every one hundred years."

Gabriela rose, her fluid movements barely making a sound as she strode toward the bookcase to admire her trophies. "Did you lose track of time?"

"I guess maybe. Two years is like a blink." She tried to snap but smeared frosting across her fingers instead.

"My assistant said the same thing when I asked her why she only brought your insubordination to my attention now. She has been reassigned to the grape pit."

Destiny swallowed hard, trying to keep her expression neutral. Turning water into wine was serious angel business, and the poor souls assigned to stomp in the grape pit had to live with purple stains up to their knees for the rest of their existences.

Gabriela whirled toward her, clutching a golden award, the silky fabric of her dress silently swishing around her ankles. "Michelle tolerates nothing less than perfection. If your misdeed goes without consequence, I can kiss my eight-time Seraph of the Decade streak goodbye. That would put my run for Seraph of the Century in jeopardy, so let me be very clear..."

She unclenched the trophy, and it floated back to its spot on the shelf. "You, my dear, sweet, little baker, will *not* be the reason I fall from Michelle's good graces. Your time on Earth is up. Pack your things and return to the angelic realm for reassignment. A few millennia in the repository should set you straight."

Destiny's heart plopped into her stomach before taking a flying leap into her throat. She was lucky she kept her mouth closed or the pint of eclair filling she'd had for breakfast would've splattered onto Gabriela's precious awards.

The repository? No. No, she couldn't let that happen. After spending over a century on Earth, she wouldn't survive down there with all those brainless cherubs and their saccharine smiles. She needed to be among the living, not that angels were dead, but whatever. Destiny needed stimulation, action, conversation...as many "tions" as she could get.

The angels who worked in the repository... Let's just say they were all a few feathers short of a full goose. They lived in the same boring building together. They did mind-numbing work together. They shared a brain cell, and it wasn't the brightest crayon in the box. If Destiny joined them, she'd be more than a few grapes short of a fruit salad too.

"I can't be a file clerk." She fisted her trembling hands and rose to her feet, her wings shuddering as she sucked in a breath. "New Orleans is teeming with recovering demons. They need me to bake the cakes that keep them in check. If I leave, it'll throw off the balance. They need me there."

"They don't need you." She waved a hand flippantly. "Anyone who knows how to follow a recipe can take on your role. *I* need you in a position where you'll have no choice but to perform every aspect of your job. A replacement will be ready by the end of the day. Someone who won't 'forget' to find miracles to perform."

"But it's *my* recipe. I created it. I perfected it." She splayed her fingers and clenched her fists again, her wings vibrating against her back. "If you give it to anyone else, I'll... I'll sue you for copyright infringement."

Gabriela's laugh sounded like a bell choir, which was infuriating. The person trying to end Destiny's life as she knew it should not have such a soothing, melodic, contagious laugh. Yet, there Destiny was, fighting with all her might not to laugh along with her exasperating boss.

"Oh, Destiny." The archangel tsked again. "You created the recipe to perform your duties under my employment. It was work for hire, so the copyright belongs to Divine Grace, Inc."

"No." Destiny shook her head. No, this could not be happening.

"It's in your contract. Did you not read it before you signed?" She waved her hand, and a cloud of golden glitter formed in the air. As it dissipated, a folder thicker than a stack of roadside diner pancakes appeared in her hand. "Would you like to read it now?"

"It's eighty-seven pages long. Of course I didn't read it all. No one does." She dropped into the chair and pressed her fingers to her temples. Arguing with an archangel would get her nowhere. Seraphs of that level were forbidden from telling lies, so if Gabriela said it was in the contract, it was in the contract.

And Destiny was screwed.

"I love New Orleans. All my friends are there." Pressure built in the back of her eyes.

Gabriela rested a hand on her shoulder, and a coolness washed through her system, calming her. "You'll make new friends in the angelic realm. You can reconnect with old ones. New Orleans hasn't always been your home."

"It feels like it has." She shrugged off her boss's soothing touch. "Assign me a miracle, and I'll perform it. Whatever it is, I'll do it. I'll scrub the muck off Bourbon Street every Sunday morning with my own toothbrush if I have to. I'll drink the whole Mississippi River and poop out the mud. I'll do anything."

"You know that's not how we operate." Gabriela sank into her chair and laid the contract on her desk. "If I had to find miracles for all my angels to perform, I would never get my paperwork done."

"Just this once?" She clasped her hands in front of her chest. "Please."

Gabriela's reproachful expression morphed into one of sympathy. "Michelle would never allow it."

"She doesn't have to know." She slapped her hand over her mouth. Did she seriously just suggest deceit? To an archangel? Oh, dear lord, she was on the fast-track to having her wings clipped with that statement. "I mean…"

Gabriela leaned forward, lowering her voice. "Michelle always knows. So do…" She pointed at the ceiling, indicating the beings even higher in status than her boss.

Destiny blinked rapidly, shaking her head. "I'm sorry. I don't... I don't know why I said that."

"You're desperate." Gabriela lifted one shoulder dismissively. "And your time on Earth has corrupted your sense of right and wrong. Returning to the angelic realm will do you good."

"No, please." She scooted to the edge of her seat. "Give me another year. I'll find a miracle to perform if it kills me."

"You haven't forgotten you're immortal, have you? Your friends there will grow old and die."

"Not all of them." She rested her fingers on the edge of the desk. "Most of my friends are immortal too. Please, Gabriela. One more year."

The archangel pressed her palms together and closed her eyes, inhaling deeply and tapping into the collective consciousness, looking for guidance, which was weird as all get out. Destiny had always assumed angels of a certain level never needed guidance. That they were the guides themselves.

Apparently, she was wrong.

A full thirty seconds passed before Gabriela opened her eyes, her mouth tightening in a perturbed expression. "I am nothing if not gracious. The higher ups tell me you do, indeed, need more time in New Orleans."

Destiny sucked in a breath. "Yes! I still have work to do there. I'll find a miracle the office will sanction before my year is up. I promise."

Gabriela shook her head. "You have three weeks."

"That's..." She started to argue that no one could get the office to sanction a miracle in that amount of time. There was a process to follow, red tape to cut. But the seraph before her had extended grace, and Destiny needed to accept what was offered. You know...gift horses and all.

"Thank you, Gabriela. I won't let you down." She rose, ready to dart out the door and find someone who needed a freaking miracle, but Gabriela closed her eyes and pressed her palms together again.

"It's no longer me with whom you'll have to contend." She pinned Destiny with a serious gaze. "This extension comes with a hefty price if you fail."

"Wh... What?" Destiny scrunched her brow. A price? Since when did angels make deals? That was the devil's department.

Gabriela waved her hand over the contract on her desk, and it morphed into a single sheet of parchment. "Michelle heard your suggestion of deceit, and she worries your time on Earth—in addition to your heredity—has corrupted you beyond repair. She feels you aren't capable of functioning in the angelic realm anymore; therefore, reassignment is no longer an option."

"But I'm an angel. I'm not corrupted." How could they say such a thing? Just because her mother gave up her wings the moment Destiny was born, it didn't mean she would follow in her freefall. Was that really what this was about? Her disgraced lineage?

A spark of anger ignited in her chest. "Have you spent any time earthbound? Do you know what it's like to be down there in the trenches?"

"Yes, though I'll admit it has been thousands of years."

"Well, let me tell you, times have changed. Temptation is everywhere. You have to learn how to exist with humans and supes alike, and not a single one of them is perfect. In my centuries there, I have remained angelic. I have guided and advised troubled souls, and I haven't once turned my back on my purpose or my duties."

"Aside from the little miracle issue."

"Aside from that." She threw her arms into the air. "Yes, I let that duty slide off my radar. It takes so dang long for the office to process miracle requests, and most of them get denied. Sometimes the rejection gets to be too much, so I went about my way, doing everything else required of me. And I'm doing a heavenly job, too, so whatever price I have to pay if I fail, I'll agree to it. Go ahead and name it, because I won't fail. Not this time."

Gabriela held her gaze for a beat, two, three, before she spoke, "The price is your wings."

"My w…" Her stomach lurched, cutting off her words.

"It's true you have done a heavenly job in New Orleans. No one is arguing otherwise. Get a miracle approved and perform it in three weeks' time, and your clock will reset, giving you another hundred years to perform your next miracle."

"And I'll keep my wings?" She drew them tightly against her back, willing them to disappear inside her like they did on Earth, but the angelic realm forbade it.

"If you succeed, yes, you'll keep them, but that is the extent of the grace being offered. If you fail, you will lose your wings, your halo, your magic, and your immortality. *You* will be the one to grow old and die while your immortal friends remain young."

Holy hummingbird cake, they were threatening to turn her human. To force her to fall like her mother had. "What if I don't accept the offer? What then?"

Gabriela sighed. "Then I say you should have accepted the repository position while it was on the table. You have no choice now. Mortality awaits you in three weeks' time. The higher ups have spoken." She offered Destiny a golden pen and turned the paper toward her. "Sign here, please."

Destiny steadied her shaking hand and pressed the pen to the page. Ink pooled around the spot, the pressure nearly tearing it as she dragged the tip down and around to form the letter D. She swallowed hard and scribbled the rest of her name on the page. The moment she finished the final E in Monroe, the pen and parchment poofed into a cloud of glitter, sealing her fate in sparkling light.

"Let's hop to it, *elfen*. Easter is in March this year, so there's no time to slack off." Pete Hasen, aka Peter Rabbit, aka Peter Cottontail—though no one better call him that to his face—stood on a wooden platform overlooking his studio. Dozens upon dozens of *elfen*, the magical critters who helped him turn faery chicken eggs into works of art, scurried about, gathering paints and brushes before settling onto their stools, ready to decorate the shipment that would be arriving shortly.

The date of Easter was tied to the lunar cycle, always falling on the Sunday after the first full moon following the spring equinox. That meant it could land on any Sunday between March 22nd and April 25th.

The month-long window of possible Sundays would freak out any Type A fae, but it didn't bother Pete. Rules, regulations, and order were never his strong suits, and how could they be? He was a fae rabbit shifter who used to be a robin. An anomaly.

Sure, he was an *elfen* robin, so he'd always been a magical being, but when the goddess Eostre decided she needed a right-hand man to bring Easter to the masses, she'd chosen Pete to do the honors.

She'd first turned him into a rabbit because it was her sacred animal, but she quickly realized a fae bunny couldn't command an army of artistic *elfen* any better than a robin could. So, she turned him into a shifter, allowing him to keep his new rabbit form to honor her while also having a human form so he could lay down the laws.

He squeezed a blob of blush pink paint onto his palette and chuckled at the memory. Laws indeed.

Artists needed freedom for their creative juices to flow. If he gave them a bunch of rules to follow, they'd freeze up and Easter would die along with their imaginations. No Easter meant no Easter

Bunny, which meant Pete would lose his job and the fluff he'd come to love.

That was why he gave his *elfen* the freedom to do as they pleased...as long as they met their quotas. He might've been the captain of this operation, but he ran a very loose ship.

He added a puddle of teal and another of lemon yellow before swirling his brush in a cup of water. The eggs always arrived like clockwork' on March 7th, giving him and his team anywhere from two to six weeks to paint, sort, and prepare them for distribution on Easter morning.

No, he did not lay the eggs himself.

Contrary to popular belief, Eostre did not give him the body parts required to attempt that feat. And thank the goddess for that. He couldn't begin to imagine the pain women went through giving birth, whether passing a living being or an unfertilized egg through a passage that was way too narrow to make it easy. He shuddered at the thought.

As he swirled a second brush in the water cup, the hairs on the back of his neck stood on end. The energy behind him shifted, vibrating and warming, and he rose to his feet, turning toward the disturbance.

Silver sparkles gathered in front of him, and a

collective gasp sounded from the *elfen* below as Eostre appeared in the mist. Pete bowed, and his *elfen* followed his lead, lowering their heads but peeking up to take in the goddess's beauty.

She had long, rose gold hair that fell in thick waves down to the small of her back, and a crown of daisies adorned her head. Her pale yellow dress shimmered as if reflecting sunlight, and her lavender eyes brightened with her smile.

"How are the egg preparations going, Peter?" She folded her hands over her stomach. "Is it safe to say there will be no scrambling this year?"

"In over sixteen hundred years, have I ever left you holding an omelet? The eggs will be painted and delivered on time, as always."

"Without a second to spare...as always?" She winked. "If I were mortal, your methods would have given me gray hair and a heart attack by now."

"Then it's a good thing you're not. Don't worry." He waved a hand dismissively. "I'll get it done."

Her brows drew together. "You do remember what will happen if you don't?"

He huffed out a laugh. "You remind me every year. I'll lose everything and become a plain old mortal robin. No more rabbit. No more human form. I'll grow old and die, et cetera. Believe me, Eostre, I love my job. I'm not going to do anything to jeopardize it or my eternal life."

"I won't have the power to maintain your immortality."

"I know. Everything will be fine." They'd had the same conversation every year, and everything had always been fine.

She held his gaze for a beat too long, her eyes tightening before she turned toward his team. "Back to work, my children. Get ready. You'll be painting more eggs than ever this year."

A few chipmunk *elfen* chittered before scurrying back to their stations, and a possum named Merideth stretched her arms over her head, revealing two tiny hands protruding from her pouch. She offered a paintbrush, and a joey's small head appeared.

Eostre laughed. "Do we have a new recruit?"

"She wanted to help," Merideth said. "I hope that's okay."

"Absolutely." The goddess turned to Pete and lowered her voice. "I think we'll need all the help we can get this year."

"How so?" He set his palette on the table next to his egg easel. "We have plenty of time."

"I've had a foreboding feeling for the past three

days." She gestured to his office and floated down the steps toward it, giving him no option but to follow.

He stopped outside the door and turned to his head *elfen*. "Max, call the henhouse and see what's taking so long. The eggs should've been delivered by now."

He stepped into the office and found Eostre leaning against his desk, holding the intricately gilded egg she'd given him after he completed the first Easter. The concern in her eyes made his stomach sink, so he closed the door to keep his team from overhearing whatever she was about to say.

"I know you worry this time of year." He shoved his hands into his pockets. "I'll try to keep the operation more organized."

"It's not the operation I'm most worried about. It's you." She set the egg on his desk and clasped her fingers.

"Me?" He tried to laugh off the sentiment, but the look on her face made his heart beat faster than Thumper's right foot. "Why?"

She parted her lips as if to speak, but she closed them again, shaking her head before repeating the gesture two more times. "I received a warning from Frigg," she finally said.

He waited for her to elaborate, but she just stared at him with pity in her eyes. No, not pity. She masked it well, but he felt a hint of fear rolling off her. "Okaaayy..." he said. "What was the warning?"

"Do you ever feel like becoming the Easter Bunny was a sacrifice?" She picked up the egg again, tracing her fingers over the golden pattern.

"It wasn't a sacrifice at all. I love who I am."

"You don't miss your old life?"

"That was over sixteen hundred years ago." He chuckled. "Honestly, I don't remember much about that time." Aside from one of Frigg's geese making up a stupid song to taunt him when Eostre first turned him into a rabbit. The tune about his cotton-tail tried to wriggle its way into his mind to play on repeat every year, and it irked him to no end.

"That can't be what she meant, then..." She tapped a finger to her lips but didn't elaborate.

He clenched his jaw. For the sake of Odin's empty eye socket, would she get to the point? If his pulse sprinted any faster, he'd shift against his will and hop right out the door. He couldn't fight his rabbit when it went into flight mode. "What did Frigg tell you? Is something going to happen to me?"

"I don't know." She flicked her gaze to his. "Perhaps I shouldn't have brought it up. You have so much work to do."

"Perhaps not, but you did." He crossed his arms. "Please tell me what she said."

She nodded, a look of resolve smoothing her features. "I met Frigg for dinner in New Orleans a few days ago. I had a craving for Antoine's Oysters Rockefeller. Have you tried them?"

"Can't say that I have." His left foot began tapping against his will, so he shifted his weight to stop the thumping.

"Something about the city, the atmosphere— and maybe the free-flowing wine—made her spout a prophecy right there in the restaurant."

His pulse slowed to a manageable speed as he took a deep breath. Frigg, the goddess of fate and motherhood, had the gift of clairvoyance. She could see into anyone's future and offer guidance if their current path in life would lead to a tragic end. It took an elaborate ceremony and tons of offerings for her to even consider a request, but when she did offer her services, the advice was clear and succinct.

Prophecies, though? Frigg never gave names, dates, or anything helpful at all when she went into her glazed-eyed, trance-like state and rattled off some obscure message she'd received from the ether.

"Ninety percent of the time, no one can figure out what she means until 'the thing' has already happened." He made air quotes. "What makes you think it applies to me?"

Eostre straightened. "The prophecy is this..."

> *Balance dies when birds lie.*
> *Forget the past. Destiny is awry.*
> *An act of hubris is all it takes*
> *to bring about the end of days.*
> *A goddess, nay, her right-hand man*
> *will leave this land to devise a plan.*
> *A sacrifice, giving up one life,*
> *can stop the war and end our strife.*
> *In Yggdrasil's name, our sacred tree,*
> *as Fate has willed it, so mote it be.*

"WELL, THAT..." He scrunched his brow and tapped his right foot. Sure, he could see why Eostre might assume it applied to him in a way, but...

"You aren't the only goddess with a 'right-hand man'. It could be about anyone."

"Yes, but most don't leave our realm, lest the angels swoop in and try to bring about Ragnarök again. *You* leave every year."

"Because it's in my job description. Santa leaves his realm every year too. Maybe the prophecy is about him and Odin."

"It specifically said 'goddess.'"

"The Tooth Faery then."

"She also works for Odin...and she's not a man."

He sighed. "'Right-hand man' is a generic term."

She raised her hands in surrender. "You're right. I shouldn't have mentioned it. I just..." She clamped her mouth shut.

"You just have a foreboding feeling. I get it." He shrugged and let his arms fall to his sides. "But let's remember not to take it literally. If she did mean me, I don't know what act of hubris I could commit. I know I'm not perfect, and no one is giving up their life on my watch."

She nodded. "Will you stay on high alert?"

"I always am." His other form was a prey animal, after all. He couldn't help but watch his back constantly.

"Mr. Hasen, sir?" Max frantically rapped on the office door. "We have a problem."

Pete opened it and found the *elfen* raccoon wringing his tiny hands. Max bounced his gaze between Pete and Eostre, his jaw trembling.

"What's the problem?" Pete squatted and rested a hand on his back.

"I called the henhouse like you asked, but...there won't be any eggs this year."

"No eggs?" Eostre tilted her head and glided toward them, unable to mask the alarm in her eyes. "Are the hens ill?"

"No, ma'am." Max wrung his hands harder. "Six of them are dead...drained of all their blood."

"How?" Pete shook his head. "Who...?"

"I don't know." Max scooted backward, out of the doorway. "What will we do?"

"Have you told anyone?" Pete asked.

"No. Not a soul."

"Keep it that way for now." He marched into the studio and climbed the steps to his platform before lifting his hands. "Attention, *elfen*. The egg delivery has been delayed. Please clean up your stations and return to your homes. I'll let you know when it's time to get started again."

The chittering turned into a murmur as the *elfen*

put away their paints. Pete hopped off the platform and made his way toward the exit, where Eostre already stood, waiting.

She took his hand, and, in a flash of magic, they appeared in front of the henhouse. Eostre didn't say a word as she ascended the ramp and tapped lightly on the door. It swung open, and she disappeared inside.

Pete swallowed hard and steeled himself before following her in. At least two dozen hens perched in their nests, some trembling, while others let out mournful clucks. Another dozen or so paced circles around the center of the room.

Eostre cleared her throat, and they all stopped, their heads snapping toward her. "Our deepest condolences for your loss. Where are the sisters who have passed?"

"Out back in the yard," a brown hen said. "Henrietta is keeping watch until Jord gets here."

"Thank you." Pete strode through the room, exiting through the back door, and Eostre followed him into the yard.

A large hen with blue-black feathers stood among the bodies, her head jerking this way and that. When her gaze landed on Eostre, she bowed. "No blood. What creature would do this?"

Pete shoved his hands into his pockets and peered at a rust-colored hen. Red marred the feathers around a tiny wound on her shoulder, but she was otherwise intact. If hungry coyotes or weasels had found their way into this realm, they'd have eaten the entire bird. He shuddered at the thought.

With just the blood missing from the bodies, it could only mean one thing.

"Vampire," Eostre said as if reading his mind. "But that's impossible. Vampires can't enter this realm."

"I don't know what else it could be." Pete stepped away from the bodies. "Someone got in somehow."

"Vampire!" Henrietta clucked, her head darting around on her neck again.

"Remain calm," Eostre said. "They cannot be out in the daylight. Your goddess, Jord, will be here soon to protect you. Peter, you must find out who did this and rid our realm of the terror."

"Me?" He raised his hands. "I'm a painter, not a fighter."

She stepped toward him and lowered her voice, gesturing to the poor hens. "'Balance dies when birds lie.' You have a vampire friend in the earthly realm, do you not?"

He ran a hand through his hair and opened his mouth to argue this was a job for the gods, but he couldn't find the words. Fae deities were forbidden from taking lives, and the *elfen* lacked the strength to battle a creature of the night. If a vampire needed staking, he had to be the man to do it.

But how the hell did a vampire get into Eostre's peaceful realm? And why go after the chickens? There were plenty of bigger *elfen* in the realm that would satiate a thirsty vamp faster than hen blood could. Nothing about this situation made any sense at all.

"My hens are too distraught to lay eggs," Henrietta said. "Some are threatening to fly the coop. If you don't help us, there'll be no Easter this year or ever again."

Nausea churned in Pete's stomach. His rabbit wanted him to open a rabbit hole, tuck tail, and bounce, but he couldn't. Not with the safety of his *elfen* and every other creature in the realm at stake. Not with his own life now hanging in the balance if Easter failed to happen.

"Peter?" Eostre rested a hand on his shoulder.

He had to be mad as a March hare to agree to

this, but what else could he do? Think of the disappointment children would feel with no eggs to hunt. And Eostre... What would happen to her if she wasn't celebrated? The gods needed offerings and celebrations in their honor to survive as much as... well, as much as vampires needed blood.

Easter had to happen. There was no way around it.

He straightened his spine, nodding with resolve. "I know a guy who can help."

CHAPTER

THREE

"This is amazing. What do you call it again?" Jane scooped a spoonful of the unconventional dessert into her mouth and closed her eyes.

Destiny smiled, her heart warming at her vampire friend's reaction to her creation. "It's called *sanguinaccio dolce* or sweet blood pudding."

"If Ethan had fed me this when he first turned me, I might've caught on to the whole blood-drinking thing a lot sooner. Mmm..." She took another bite and brushed her long, brown hair behind her shoulder.

"You're supposed to make it with pig's blood." Destiny spooned a serving into a blue ceramic bowl and set it on the counter. "It took a while for

Gaston to convince me to try it with human blood."

The senior vampire drummed his fingers on the countertop. "And now it sells like warm pies—"

"Hotcakes," Jane said.

Gaston arched a brow. "Like *hotcakes* to the vampire community, does it not?"

"It does, and as long as I'm using bagged blood that's been voluntarily donated, I don't mind making it." She pushed the bowl toward him.

"I will wait for my guest to arrive."

"Okay." Destiny returned the serving container to the fridge. "Where are Maeve and Ethan tonight?"

Gaston strolled toward a glass case filled with mini bundt cakes and tarts and peered at Destiny's creations. "Maeve is tending to her bats at the sanctuary, and Ethan is crisping numerals at Jane's club."

"Crunching numbers," she said around a mouthful of pudding. "He gets ornerier than a bear with its butt shaved when he's balancing the books. I keep my distance during his monthly cycle."

"Perhaps if you didn't watch over his shoulder the entire time..." Gaston said.

"Meh. It's fine." Jane waved off his comment.

"I'll take care of him when he gets home. His stress melts away when Vlad the Impaler gets to do his thing." She wiggled her eyebrows and took another bite of pudding. "What's got your halo off-kilter, Destiny? You're not your usual self."

"Is it that obvious?" She wiped her hands on a towel before dishing up three slices of her famous demon-subduing angel food cake with strawberry sauce for an online order. "Where's your friend, Gaston? Does he know how to get here?"

"He should be *hopping* in at any moment." He smirked as if he'd just told a joke.

Jane laughed. "Hippity Hoppity. He's on his way."

Destiny cut her gaze between the vampires as they shared a laugh, but she didn't dare ask what it was about. Knowing them, she probably didn't want to know.

Gaston sat in a yellow chair at a lavender table, his black trench coat and boots contrasting with the pastels she'd decorated her bakery with. "After the Santa debacle, I can't believe I allowed Jane to attend this reunion. Perhaps my better judgment is waning with my age."

Jane rolled her eyes. "A girl makes one tiny mistake that almost ruins Christmas, and he'll never let me live it down." She plopped into the chair next to him. "I promise not to run him over. Easter won't be ruined on my watch."

"Easter?" Destiny tilted her head. "Is the friend you're meeting the...?"

"The Easter Bunny?" Jane rubbed her palms together. "Yep. In the fluff."

Destiny's mouth dropped open. "Wow. That's... How do you know him?"

Gaston waved a hand flippantly. "He's a friend from the old days. I haven't seen him in over one hundred years, so when he reached out, of course, I dropped everything to meet with him."

"Hmm." Destiny lowered her gaze. "Over one hundred years." That sounded familiar.

She swiped open her phone to double-check the online order. "Oh, shoot. The angel food cake was supposed to be a go order."

"I'll help you box it up, and you can tell me your woes." Jane glided behind the counter and picked up a plate. "Receive some help instead of giving it for a change."

"These are trash. They'll get soggy before the demons can eat them. I'll have to put the sauce in a separate container." She checked the order again. "I could have sworn it said they wanted to eat them here."

"Maybe they changed it," Jane said.

"Maybe." Destiny dumped the contents of one plate into the trash and spun around for the second one. Jane turned at the same time, and they smacked into each other, the plate Jane held smashing onto Destiny's chest, covering her lemon-yellow sundress in strawberry sauce.

"Oh, my goat cheese. I'm so sorry." Jane scraped what was left of the cake into the trash and set the plate in the sink. "You can like...miracle it away, right?" She waved her hand over the stain.

Destiny laughed dryly. "I'm an angel, not a magician."

She wiped the mess with a dishtowel, and the bells above the front door chimed. Without looking up, she said, "Hi. Welcome to Sweet Destiny's," in the most cheerful voice she could muster.

"How can I help—" She lifted her gaze and dropped the towel, completely losing the ability to speak or breathe as her eyes locked with his.

The man, the myth, the frigging Easter Bunny, stood about six feet tall. His wavy, brown hair looked like the kind of messy do that he either woke up with or spent half an hour mastering each morning. It didn't matter which, because his jewel-green eyes literally sparkled as one side of his mouth tugged into a crooked smile.

Hark, the herald angels. She couldn't tear her gaze away. She had no clue how long she stood there, grinning like an idiot, and she didn't care. This man was... Well, he was *something*.

Finally, he broke eye contact, but he didn't look away. No, he let his gaze meander over her face, down her body, and back to her eyes before widening his smile. "Hi. I'm Pete."

"You're the Easter Bunny." She clamped her mouth shut. Why she felt the need to tell the man who he was, she couldn't say. *Of course he knows who he is, silly. Get it together.*

He chuckled. "And you're Sweet Destiny, I presume?"

Her cheeks heated. "Just Destiny."

"Why do I get the feeling there isn't anything 'just' about you?" He held her gaze for a beat or two before glancing at her dress. "It's a pleasure to meet you."

Jane handed her a wet towel, and her stomach sank as the mortification set in. His meandering gaze hadn't been one of admiration like she'd thought. He'd seen her current disheveled state and had judged her accordingly.

"I'm sorry. I'm not usually a mess." Okay, that was a lie. Ever since her meeting with Gabriela at Divine Grace, she'd been nothing short of a dumpster fire.

She wiped her dress, but it only smeared the stain more. "This is so unprofessional of me. I don't normally look like..."

"Honestly, I didn't even notice." He shoved his hands into his pockets and shrugged, and she could have sworn his eyes sparkled again.

The heat on her cheeks spread down her neck, no doubt turning her chest bright red. "I'm going to change. I'll be right back."

She ducked into the kitchen and leaned against a counter, pinching the bridge of her nose as she reminded herself to breathe. So what if a mouthwatering immortal legend stood in the front of her bakery? He hadn't come to see her; he was meeting Gaston.

But he had seen her looking like the Hot Mess Express, and that just would not do. Angels had a level of perfection they were expected to live up to, and Destiny hadn't just missed the mark...she'd smeared strawberry syrup all over it.

"I sure as hell hope you're both single because the energy between you two is off the charts hot." Jane grabbed a stack of go boxes and folded three. "I didn't see any more angel food cake out front. Do you have any back here?"

"It's in the walk-in." She tilted her head back to stare at the ceiling, wishing a portal would open up and whisk her away. Maybe she should have taken that assignment in the repository after all. "Don't eat any. It tempers demonic powers. I don't know what it would do to a vampire."

"I'll stick to the sweet blood pudding." Jane retrieved the cake and put three slices into boxes. "Aren't you going to change?"

"I can't go back out there. He thinks I'm a mess."

She stacked the boxes and rested a hand on top. "He thinks you're the most heavenly creature he's ever laid eyes on."

"No, he doesn't. He saw me for what I am: a dumpster fire."

Jane squinted. "Read the room, woman. I think time actually stood still out there for a moment or two. You glowed, girl. Golden light emanated from your pores, and I'm pretty sure he heard a choir of angels singing the moment he looked at you."

Destiny tugged on her lower lip. "You think?"

"I know. I saw his eyes literally sparkle. The Easter Bunny has the hots for you, and you know what they say about rabbits..." She wiggled her brows. "Go change and get back out there. Your bunny hole will thank you later."

Butterflies took flight in Destiny's stomach at the thought. If Jane felt the chemistry between them, maybe she hadn't imagined it. She pushed from the counter, ready to follow her friend's advice, when reality sank in. "I can't. He's an immortal fae, and I've only got two weeks left."

"Two weeks left for what? Where are the sauce cups?"

"Second shelf from the top." She hadn't told a soul about her predicament. A full week had passed since Gabriela had given her the ultimatum, and Destiny had put in two miracle requests so far. The first one had been auto-rejected, which was no surprise. The gator shifter who'd asked for help had wagered his left nut in a deal with Satan fair and square. Yes, it would take a miracle to get it back, but angels weren't in the business of helping people renege on deals with the devil.

The second made it through the initial screen, which meant it was currently sitting in the new assistant's inbox, and heaven knew how long it would be there. Housing all the unhoused in New Orleans probably wouldn't get approved either. It was too big of an ask.

She inhaled and blew out a hard breath. "I have two weeks to get a miracle approved and perform it."

Jane tilted her head. "You're an angel. That's easy-peasy, right? Don't you perform miracles every day?"

"No, and that's the problem." She ran a dish-towel under the faucet and dabbed it on her dress. "I can perform small acts of magic, but it takes months to get an actual miracle approved."

"Why does it take so long? And why do you have to get them approved?"

The stain refused to budge, so she tossed the towel onto the counter. "Because miracles are life-altering and angels thrive on helping others. If we went all willy-nilly and changed people's lives on the daily, they'd never learn to take responsibility for themselves."

"That makes sense, I guess." Jane poured sauce into three plastic cups. "What happens if you're late?"

"I'll lose my wings and my immortality. I'll be a regular human, grow old, and die." She threw her hands into the air. "So you see why I can't get it on with an immortal bunny? What would be the point?" No matter how hot a fire he lit inside her.

Jane snapped lids onto the sauce cups. "Why did they only give you two weeks if it takes months?"

Destiny dug her fingers into the back of her neck, working out the tension. "They gave me three. I'm already one week in."

Jane added the cups to the cake boxes and crossed her arms. "And you haven't asked anyone for help, have you?"

"How can I? This is my problem. I slacked off, and now I have to pay the price."

"Destiny, honey. That's not how friendship works. We're going to find you a miracle to perform, and we'll get it approved if I have to fly up to heaven on a reindeer and hold your boss at fang point."

"Divine Grace is in the angelic realm, not heaven."

"Wherever I have to go." She took Destiny's shoulders in her hands. "You're not alone, okay?"

"You don't need to get involved. I'm sure you've got plenty on your plate." She pressed her fingers to her temples.

"My plate is huge and made of industrial-strength polycarbonate. Load it up."

Destiny drew in a shaky breath, remembering how it felt when people refused her help. Acts of service was her love language. How could she deny her friend expressing the same kind of love?

She flashed a grateful smile. "Thank you, Jane. I don't know how you can help, but I do appreciate the support."

"Good. Now, go change and get your celestial ass back out there. Your future snuggle bunny is waiting."

Her stomach fluttered, but her smile faded. "There's another problem, though. He's a fae."

"So?"

"Faeries and angels don't exactly get along. We've been at odds for millennia. Sometimes even at war."

"Uh-huh. So, you don't like him because he's a different species?"

"I never said I didn't like him."

"Then why are you sabotaging your chances before you even get to know him?" Jane wagged a finger. "And don't you dare say it's because he saw you looking imperfect."

Destiny sighed. "I don't know."

"Satan's balls, woman. Go. Change."

"I..." She clamped her mouth shut before she

could utter another excuse. Her friend was right. She was self-sabotaging, which was no surprise. She needed to focus on her miracle, but maybe...just maybe...Fate had sent the Easter Bunny to help her figure it out.

And why not? Stranger things had happened in this town.

Destiny grinned. "I know just the dress."

FOUR

"A vampire is the only thing that could have done it." Pete sank a fork into the slice of cake Destiny had left on the counter for him. The strawberry sauce, not overly sweet, complemented the light, spongy texture perfectly. It had also complemented the buttery yellow color of her dress.

His stomach tightened as an image of the heavenly woman flashed in his mind. She was beautiful beyond comparison. Anyone would attest to that, but there was so much more to her. A connection on a level deeper than he ever thought possible. He had felt it the moment their eyes met.

And how did she know angel food cake was his favorite?

"I suppose a newly undead might turn to poultry blood without proper guidance." Gaston's voice drew him from his thoughts. "But it's a rare vampire who can cross into that realm. Are you certain there isn't a species of fae who might do such a thing? An *elfen* chupacabra, perhaps?" He scooped a spoonful of his dessert into his mouth and closed his eyes for a long blink. "Or someone making *sanguinaccio dolce*, perhaps?"

"No fae would kill six chickens to make pudding." Pete took another bite of cake, savoring the melding of flavors on his tongue.

Gaston laced his fingers and rested his hands on the table. "You have too much faith in people. Even the fae can go rogue."

"I suppose that's true, though I can't fathom it. But you're right about vampires not being able to cross into our realm. A fae would have to invite them over, and that's even more unfathomable." He laughed as he used his last bite to soak up as much sauce from the plate as possible. "Says the man who's about to invite the Magistrate's right-hand vamp to cross over."

"Perhaps the culprit didn't need an invitation," Gaston said.

"Only a person with fae blood can cross into

Eostre's realm uninvited. I don't know any fae vampires."

"I do."

Pete scratched his head, a fog forming in his brain as he took the last bite of angel food cake. Why were they talking about vampires? And what did vamps have to do with the fae? He blinked rapidly and stared at the plate in front of him. The remnants of a pinkish-red sauce were smeared across the pastel blue surface, reminding him of... something.

He flicked his gaze to the man sitting across from him. His aura screamed powerful vampire, sending his heart into a sprint. Why the hell was he having dessert with a vampire?

And since when did vampires eat food?

His knee bounced of its own volition, so he pressed his palm on his thigh to stop it. How did he get here? Where was he? More importantly...

Who was he?

"Are you not going to ask who I mean?" The vampire smirked. "It's a rather *jolly* story."

"Who?" he muttered, though he wasn't inquiring about the story. He could not, for the life of him, remember his own name.

"Santa Claus himself," the vampire said. "My

dear friend Jane ran him over with my beloved Maserati, Genevieve. She had no choice but to turn him."

"I don't..." He rubbed his forehead. Santa Claus was a vampire? How was that relevant to their conversation...whatever it was they were talking about?

"Pete?" the vampire said, and he snapped his gaze to meet his ice-blue eyes. "Peter, are you okay?" Concern carved lines into the man's forehead.

"Peter..." he mumbled. Apparently, that was his name. "I'm fine."

Yes, that was a lie. His heart thumped so fast, it threatened to crack his rib cage, and his left foot tapped repeatedly, his rabbit instinct begging him to shift and hop out of there. He was about to do just that when an ethereal woman stepped through the kitchen door.

Her copper hair shimmered as she moved, and she wore a knee-length dress with pastel stripes that reminded him of... He couldn't remember what it reminded him of, but it sure as sugar felt right.

Another woman entered behind her, this one a brunette vampire carrying three pastry boxes. He glanced at her before locking his gaze on the angel's sky-blue eyes. They brightened when she smiled, tempering the panic that threatened to take over his entire being.

"Holy goat cheese pizza," the brunette said. "Gaston, tell me you didn't feed that cake to the Easter Bunny."

What an odd thing to say. The angel's eyes widened as she flicked her gaze to the empty plate in front of him. She snapped her head toward the counter and then back at his plate before snatching it off the table.

"Oh, no. No, no, no. Pete, did you eat the angel food cake?"

His shoulders crept toward his ears. "Maybe?" It was an honest answer, but apparently not the one they wanted to hear. The energy in the room grew palpable: wariness, concern, worry tipping toward panic.

His hands trembled with the urge to shift, so he fisted them. "Was I not supposed to?"

"No!" The angel set the plate on the counter and whirled toward him. "Are you okay? Tell me how you feel. What's different?"

"I feel..." He sensed her panic, the brunette's worry, the man's confusion. As for himself? "I don't know."

The man rose and carried his bowl to the

counter, setting it next to the empty plate. "The cake was here, next to my dish. I assumed you set it out for Pete."

"Oh, dear." The angel wrung her hands. "That was meant for a demon. I don't know what it will do to him."

"Oh, dear, indeed." The man arched a brow at Pete. "Are you okay, *mon ami?*"

"I don't..." His gaze darted from the man to the brunette to the angel. "Who are you people?"

"I'm Jane." The brunette approached him with slow, cautious steps. "This is Gaston and Destiny. You know that, right? You met us twenty minutes ago."

No, he did not. He'd never seen these strangers in his life. At least...he didn't think he had. His brain was fuzzier than his tail at the moment.

Jane took another step toward him, and he shot to his feet. "What did you do to me? Why am I here?" Where else should he be?

"Oh, sweet spirits. This is bad." Destiny's voice drew his gaze to her. Something about her presence calmed him, called to him...to his rabbit. But what was an angel doing colluding with vampires?

"What's the last thing you remember?" she asked.

"I don't know. I..." He racked his brain, trying his damnedest to conjure a memory, finding nothing but a blank slate. A rabbit hole leading to a bottomless pit. "I can't remember anything."

"Do you know who you are?" she asked.

He glanced at Jane and Gaston before returning his gaze to hers. "I assume my name is Pete, since that's what you're calling me."

"Dude, you're the Easter Bunny," Jane said.

A maniacal laugh rolled up from his chest. "Yeah, right. And you're the Tooth Fairy. And I suppose that's Santa Claus." He waved a hand at Gaston.

His body hummed with the need to shift. These people were more than a few eggs short of a dozen. They looked at each other with strange expressions and scrunched their brows at him.

"What's going on?" he asked. "What did you do to me?"

"Destiny," Jane said, "I think we know how your cake affects the fae now."

The fae? Was this some kind of sick joke? He was a rabbit shifter, not a fae, and definitely not the fluffing Easter Bunny.

The angel buried her face in her hands and took a deep breath before tilting her head toward the ceiling. "Good gracious. I gave the Easter Bunny amnesia."

"You're insane. All of you. Stop calling me that." He shuddered, every hair on his body standing on end, his skin threatening to sprout fur.

"Pete," Destiny took a step toward him. "It's who you are."

Something about the way she said it made him want to believe it was true, but he shook his head, chasing away the feeling. She was an angel. Who knew what kind of power she had over people's minds. She'd obviously blanked his. Or maybe the vampires had.

"No." He backed toward the door. "Whatever this is, I want no part of it. I'm out."

He shoved the door open, shifted into his rabbit form, and darted away. Where he should go, he had no clue, but anywhere was better than there.

DESTINY'S MOUTH hung open as the door slowly swung back, the click of the latch sounding so final, her wings nearly molted right there in the shop. They might as well have. Her halo could have clattered on the floor for all it mattered.

Michelle tolerates nothing less than perfection. Gabriela's words rang in her ears. This fiasco was nothing less than an epic fail.

"Let it be known that Jane Devereaux did not have a hand in ruining Easter." Jane locked the front door and rested her hands on her hips. "I'll own the Santa debacle, but this was all you, Gaston."

His eyes flashed with menace, and he straightened to his full height, his aura pulsing with power. The last thing Destiny needed was a vampire fight in her bakery. Not when she'd just committed the flub to end all flubs.

Or life as she knew it, at least.

"It's not Gaston's fault." She plopped into a chair and dropped the magic masking her wings and halo. She didn't have the energy to keep up the charade.

"You see?" He gestured at her. "It's not my fault."

Jane snorted. "You know how the demons stay tame. You didn't stop to think the cake might've been magical?"

"Why would I? It was sitting right next to my pudding." He crossed his arms.

"It was a mistake. He didn't know." Destiny

dropped her elbows on the table and held her head in her hands. "I'll lose my wings over this for sure."

"No, you won't." Jane sank into the seat across from her. "And speaking of wings...wow! If perfection had a poster child, you would be it. I've never seen you in all your angelic gloriousness."

Destiny forced out a sardonic laugh and laid her arms on the table. "I'm the farthest from perfect an angel can be. I gave the frigging Easter Bunny amnesia. I don't deserve wings. Or this." She gestured at the golden ring floating atop her head.

"It's not your fault." Jane rested a hand on hers.

"I left the cake there. It's my fault."

Jane pursed her lips. "You only left it there because I smashed a plate onto your dress. If I'd been more careful, you wouldn't have rushed into the kitchen."

"So you do take responsibility..." Gaston teased.

Jane stuck out her tongue. "I'm just saying that a string of events led to Pete's brain turning into a dust bunny. You didn't force-feed him. Surely, your boss will see that."

She shrugged. "So what if she does? Easter will be here in a few weeks. How will that work without the Easter Bunny?"

"The same way Christmas would have worked

without Santa. It won't." Gaston stood with his hands behind his back, staring out the window. "You will have to remedy the situation quickly. Pete was already on a mission to save Easter."

"It needed saving *before* I blanked his mind?"

"Several fae hens have been murdered. Drained of blood. The rest aren't laying eggs." Gaston turned toward them. "That is why he traveled here. He needed help."

"Hot damn." Jane slapped her hand on the table. "The timing couldn't be more perfect."

Destiny's eye twitched. No eggs, no antidote for angel magic, a bunny who was MIA. "I don't see—"

"Think about it. After everything that happened, what will it take to save Easter?"

She lifted a hand and dropped it on the table. "A mira...cle." She sucked in a sharp breath. "It'll take a miracle."

Jane flashed a conspiratorial grin. "And I know just the angel to make it happen."

Could this be it? The thing that would save her immortality? Easter in peril was way more important than a gator shifter's left testicle. It was certainly miracle-worthy.

"You're right." Unable to fight her smile, she

rose and tucked her chair under the table. "They can't possibly reject saving Easter."

Jane swiped her phone screen. "It's three weeks away."

"And I have two." She bounced on her toes, a giddy sensation expanding in her stomach.

"You've got this, sister." Jane stood, joining in her excitement.

Destiny strode behind the counter and opened her laptop. The keys clicked at lightning speed beneath her fingers as she filled out the miracle request form. She hit enter and closed the computer. "*We've* got this."

"How can I help?" Jane asked.

She activated her glamour, hiding her wings and halo. "First things first. We have to find Pete."

What in Odin's name? Pete hunkered down beneath a bush outside a two-story brick house with white columns and green shutters. A chill hung in the night air, making his fur stand on end, but the cold didn't stop the mass of people from gathering along the street as a parade of lights, colors, and festive sounds rolled by.

A marching band stopped in front of him to break it down to a funky drum beat while masked women atop a double-decker float covered in flowers threw beads and plastic doubloons to the spectators below.

He'd somehow ended up in New Orleans. That

much was obvious from the architecture and revelry. *How* he'd gotten there, he had no clue. Had he come with friends for a vacation? If so, where were they? *Who* were they?

Definitely not the vampires in the bakery. He'd never seen those two in his life. The angel, though...

His body had reacted to her in a way his mind couldn't comprehend. It felt as if he knew her...or he was supposed to know her. More than that, though, it felt as if he were there in that bakery *for* her.

He wrinkled his nose, wiggling his whiskers and backing deeper into the bush. He didn't know his head from his fuzzy ass at the moment, so how could he possibly believe he'd come all the way to New Orleans to meet an angel?

And all the way from where?

At the moment, it didn't matter. His head throbbed, his eyes watered, and if his stomach didn't stop lurching, he was sure to hack up whatever he'd eaten in the angel's bakery. What had she called it? Demon cake?

No, it was probably devil's food cake.

He closed his eyes and wiped away the moisture with his paw. With the way things were going, it would be his luck to wake up with them crusted shut.

A rustling in the bushes made his ears twitch. He flared his nostrils, breathing deeply and nearly choking on the stench of cat pee. A tomcat lurked somewhere in the row of hedges where Pete was hiding, and it had just sprayed a fence seconds before he decided to take a big breath. *Gross.*

He flattened his ears against his body and froze to assess his choices. If the cat caught him in his current state, he'd become a gourmet dinner for the feline. He could turn tail and run before it found him, but he had no idea how fast the creature could sprint. His other option would be to shift into his human form and walk away.

A low growl emanated from the third bush to his left, and his heart took off in a sprint. His legs should have followed suit, but he remained frozen to the spot, his gaze darting back and forth as the cat prowled closer.

The house had cameras covering the entire front porch and yard. If he shifted right there in the bushes, they'd have his face on film and an arrest warrant issued before sunrise. He'd never recover his memory sitting in a jail cell, and that meant flight was the only viable option.

Now if he could just get his feet to move.

The cat made a deep mewling sound, and as a

spotlight from a parade float flashed toward them, its eyes glowed green. Pete's foot thumped twice before his muscles obeyed the command from his brain.

He shot out of the bush faster than a greased pig at a livestock auction and high-tailed it across the yard. The cat gave chase, darting after him as he hung a right on the next street. The frigging houses had cameras on every corner, making it impossible for him to shift, so he hopped as fast as he could toward the cemetery in the distance.

He dared a peek over his shoulder, but the cat had vanished. Slowing his pace, he clung to the shadows, listening, breathing, searching for signs of his would-be attacker.

"Aw! A kitty!" A woman stumbled down the street, and Pete scooted closer to the building. "Here kitty, kitty."

She stepped into the side yard, but her friend grabbed her wrist. "You can't go into people's gardens, Sam."

Pete glanced at where the woman gestured and found the cat perched on a windowsill. It narrowed its eyes, its fur standing in a ridge along its back as it hissed and darted away.

Relief made Pete's breath come out in a rush, and he continued his trek toward the cemetery. He made it inside the gates and found an empty flower urn to hide in. Snuggling inside, he closed his eyes and willed the pounding in his head to stop.

He had nowhere to go and no money to rent a room, so he stayed in rabbit form and settled in for the night. Maybe tomorrow his headache would ease and he could think straight. Maybe he'd wake up and remember who he was.

The Easter Bunny, my fluffy, brown ass. He blew out a hard breath and closed his eyes.

Soft morning sunlight painted the back of his eyelids red, and he blinked them open, peeking his head out of the urn. Rows and rows of above-ground tombs extended from the foggy earth. Some of them sported white stucco with urns filled with fake flowers while others stood crumbling, years of neglect washing away the paint, revealing the brick and mortar beneath.

He shivered, the chilly air making his fur stand on end, and he stood on his hind legs, resting his front paws on the rim of the urn. His ears twitched, turning this way and that, as he listened for signs of predators.

Eerie stillness greeted his senses as he hopped from his makeshift bed and ducked behind a tomb. With no cameras in sight, he shifted, stretching his arms over his head. A splotch of pink paint marred the sleeve of his dark green sweater.

Odd. He couldn't remember painting anything.

He sighed and rubbed the sleep from his eyes. Of course he didn't remember painting anything. He couldn't remember *any* anything.

Maybe a walk around town would jog his memory. He made his way to the cemetery gates, but they were locked. A quick glance at his watch told him it was only seven A.M. No one would be around to open the gates for another three hours.

He tilted his head, studying the padlock on the chain, and the strange notion that locks could never keep him out made his brow furrow. Cradling the culpable object in his palm, he rested his other hand atop it. Without so much as a twitch of his nose, the lock disengaged, and the gate swung open.

"How about that?" He stepped through and locked it behind him. Shifters didn't normally possess extra powers beyond their animals' instincts, so his newfound ability had him pondering. Could he be part witch? Or maybe he had some kind of magical lock-picking artifact? Possibly his watch or something in his pocket?

He patted the front and back of his pants but found them empty. His watch had to be magical. It was the only explanation. He felt his rabbit in his soul. If he had witch blood pumping through his veins, he surely would've felt that too.

The rising sun tamed the chill in the morning air, and he tipped his head back, letting it warm his cheeks for a moment before hanging a right and making his way toward the French Quarter. He would find some shifters—preferably rabbits—and hope to hell someone could tell him who the fluff he really was.

"WE SEARCHED HALF THE NIGHT. Where could he be?" Destiny wrung her hands and rocked back and forth in the chair across from the high priestess's desk.

Crimson's dark brown hair hung in ringlets down to her shoulders, and lines formed on her forehead as she frowned. "You lost the Easter Bunny?"

"Yes!" Destiny flung her arms into the air. "I

mean, technically, he hopped away, but he doesn't know who he is, he's in a strange city, he's helpless."

Crimson drummed her manicured nails on the desk. "Strange city, I'll give you, but I highly doubt a hundreds-of-years-old fae is helpless."

"He doesn't know he's a fae. He didn't even know his name. Can you do a scrying spell or something?" Before she could answer, Destiny's phone pinged with a notification from Divine Grace. "Oh, thank heaven. If my miracle got approved, I can just…"

Her shoulders slumped with her sinking heart. "Auto-rejected. You have got to be kidding me. What the heck is Article C-37?"

"Talk to me, hon." Crimson rose and walked around her desk before leaning her backside against the edge. "What happened?"

Destiny laughed dryly. "I'm a fuck up. That's what happened."

Crimson raised her brows. "I think that might be the first time I've ever heard you cuss."

"I can't seem to do anything else right, so why not?" She pressed her hands together and inhaled deeply, attempting to connect with the collective consciousness for guidance. Relaxing her body, she focused inward, letting the world slip away before she turned her attention to the ether.

Normally, a warm light and a soft vibration would greet her, allowing her to sift through the sands of wisdom to find the answers she needed. Now, no ethereal luminescence warmed her soul, and not even a quick buzz danced through her psyche. It was as if someone had unplugged her.

She sighed heavily and opened her eyes. "I don't know what's wrong with me."

"Nothing is wrong with you." Crimson sank into the chair next to her and rested a hand atop hers. "Believe me, I'm the queen of fuck ups, and you don't belong anywhere in my queendom. No one expects you to be perfect."

"Gabriela does." She dragged a hand down her face. "Then there's Michelle."

She explained her predicament, how she missed the deadline to perform a miracle, and the ridiculous timeline Gabriela had given her. "I thought, surely, restoring Pete's memories so he can save Easter would be a miracle-worthy endeavor. Apparently, Article C-37 says otherwise."

"Come with me." Crimson's heels clicked on the hardwood as she strode from the coven office and headed to the kitchen. "What's Article C-37? What did you put on the form?"

Destiny followed and sat on a stool at the island. "I told them the Easter Bunny has amnesia, and I would like permission to perform the miracle of restoring his memories and saving Easter. I don't know what that article says. I'll have to look it up."

Crimson filled a copper bowl with water before sprinkling in dried herbs from the cabinet. "It sounds to me like you asked for two miracles. Restoring his memory *and* saving Easter. Maybe that's why it got rejected."

"You could be right. The whole reason he came to New Orleans was to get Gaston's help. Easter was already in peril before he met me." Destiny rolled her head from side to side, stretching the tension in her neck. "Crap. I did ask for two miracles. C-37 must mean only one request per form."

"Revise the request and just ask to 'save Easter'." Crimson returned the herb jars to the cabinet. "He'll get his memory back in the process. Two birds, one stone. *Voila.* Problem solved."

"I can't revise it. I have to start over from scratch, and I don't even know if that's the problem."

"Then start over. Doing nothing gets you

nowhere." She rummaged through a drawer and pulled out two candles, one pink, one baby blue. "To channel Easter vibes." She lit the wicks and set them on either side of the bowl before holding a crystal pendulum above it.

Destiny's phone pinged again, and she closed her eyes. "I can't handle any more bad news."

"You better check it," Crimson said. "Maybe someone found him."

She swiped open the screen to find an email from Gabriela. The subject line read *A few things you should know.*

"Oh, dear lord. What else?" She opened the email and read the message aloud, "'Dearest Destiny. In light of your recent debacle and your ridiculous miracle request, we have placed a new stipulation on your redemption. You may no longer use your magic until your miracle is approved.'"

Crimson stopped scrying and lowered the pendulum to the counter. "What's ridiculous about saving Easter?"

"There's more. 'Your wings and halo have been bound. Whether it's temporary or permanent is up to you. From this point forward, all your powers have been stripped. If you had read the angel hand-book, you would know Article C-37 states that no angel may request a miracle to remedy their own mistake. I'm disappointed in you, Destiny. Fix it and do better or suffer the consequences. Warm regards, Gabriela.'"

"Warm regards, my tush." She laid her phone face-down on the counter and pressed her fingers to her temples. "I knew that. I knew I couldn't fix my own mistake with a miracle, but for a moment, I thought perhaps it wasn't my fault. I'm not the one who gave him the cake, but it's my fault, nonetheless. I left it out."

Crimson pursed her lips, giving Destiny a look that said she wasn't buying it. "It was a mistake. Your boss admitted that in the email. Intention is everything, and your intent was not for him to eat it."

"Intention doesn't matter. I'm basically mortal now, Pete still has amnesia, and who knows what will happen to him if Easter is ruined. I am an epic failure."

"No, you're not, and I don't want to hear that cross your lips again." She held the pendulum over the bowl again, swinging it in circles around the edge. "You might not be able to use your magic, but your friends can. We're going to help you."

The pendulum swung in tighter and tighter

circles before it stopped in the center, buzzing like a vibrator with brand-new batteries. *Plunk.* It dropped into the water, and Crimson's eyes widened.

"What does that mean?" Destiny asked.

Crimson rested her hands on the counter. "It means he's here."

"Witches." Pete stood outside the gate of the dark blue, nineteenth-century Victorian and crossed his arms. Pots overflowing with ferns hung from the coven house's eaves, and magenta bougainvillea blooms filled the flowerbeds in front of the structure, creating a welcoming vibe.

Still, he hesitated to enter.

"I promise you, if there is anyone in New Orleans who can help you remember, it's Crimson." Sophie, the blonde wolf shifter he'd found walking dogs in the French Quarter, stood by his side and rested a hand on his shoulder.

She had a calming, magical energy about her, and it almost felt as if she could talk to his rabbit directly, even while he was in human form. It was why he'd chosen to trust her, despite all logic. Her animal could have his for breakfast in a heartbeat, but she was the first and only shifter in the city his rabbit hadn't forced him to flee from.

He'd scoured The Crescent City, searching for anyone like him, rabbit, hare, hell...he'd have settled for a nutria shifter...but all he'd found were predators.

The gator shifter behind the bar at Lafitte's Blacksmith Shop looked like he'd wanted to eat him, and the pair of bobcat sisters he'd found playing music in Jackson Square had enough menace roiling in their auras to make him do an about-face and duck into a praline shop.

When Sophie had approached him with a pack of chihuahuas, his mind had told him to bolt. The vicious little hellhounds normally would have turned into a yip-yapping frenzy at the first whiff of rabbit, but she'd kept them under control as she'd approached, and her demeanor had him spilling his guts—the parts he could recall—within the first two minutes of their conversation.

She patted his back and strode up the walk, stopping and turning when he didn't follow. "What's the matter, hon?"

"You're sure you can't point me to the local rabbit herd? Witches can mess with my mind as easily as vampires and angels."

Sophie laughed and strode toward him, linking her arm through his. "If the vampires and angel you described are who I think they are, you can bet your fuzzy bunny balls they didn't do this to you. Now, come on. The high priestess is a friend of mine."

She tugged him up the walk, and he did his best not to drag his feet. Sophie rang the doorbell, keeping a tight hold on his arm. They waited and waited. When no one answered, she used the knocker, tapping the metal loop against the wood.

"They might all be at their day jobs." She tried the knob, but it was locked. "Crimson should be here at least. She's probably upstairs or something. I'll call her."

Pete eyed the deadbolt. *I wonder...* He pressed his palm to the lock, and the mechanism clunked as it disengaged. Sophie's brow pinched as she watched him reach for the knob. It turned freely, and he pushed open the door.

"You look just as perplexed as I feel," she said, cutting her gaze between him and the open door.

"I don't know how I do it." He shrugged.

"Hmm..." Sophie furrowed her brow at him

before peeking her head inside. "Hey, Crim? You there?"

"Coming," a melodic voice drifted toward them, followed by two sets of footsteps.

"Pete. Oh, thank goodness." Destiny sashayed toward him, wearing a light pink dress with white flowers, and before he could react to her presence, she flung her arms around him, pulling him into a tight hug.

A cooling calmness flushed through his system, making him feel like all was right in the world, yet nothing about it felt ethereal. In fact, he didn't feel an ounce of magic radiating from her body as she embraced him, which was odd as all get out. When he'd met her in the bakery, he could feel her angelic power from across the room.

His nose brushed her soft, copper hair, and he inhaled against his will, breathing in the scents of lavender and vanilla. An ache formed in his chest, the sensation of longing making his stomach clench. But longing for what? He didn't know this woman, yet she felt so familiar to him.

"I thought I'd lost you." She pulled away and clutched his shoulders. "Come inside. We have work to do."

"It's okay," Sophie said. "Nothing to be afraid of."

Not when it came to Destiny, it seemed. As she backed through the doorway, he searched her aura for the silver and gold angelic glow he'd witnessed in the bakery, but it was gone. She appeared completely mundane.

No, that wasn't the right word. Nothing about her was mundane or ordinary in any way, but he couldn't detect even a hint of magic about her. She beckoned him inside, and his body reacted, taking a step toward the door before he realized he was moving.

He couldn't say why, but the feeling that he'd follow this woman anywhere burrowed deep into his chest, taking root in his heart. He lifted his leg to take another step when Sophie rested her hand on his back. She didn't try to push him forward physically, but the warm, fuzzy, controlling magic seeping from her palm was unmistakable. Was that why he'd trusted her? Because she was coercing him, and he'd been too distraught to notice it? *Oh, hell no.*

He sidestepped and pivoted, shrugging off her enchanted touch. "I need you to stop it with the magic. I may not know my ears from the fluff on my toes, but I do know I don't like to be controlled."

She raised her hands. "Fuck me with a broomstick. I was only trying to help. You said yourself your rabbit makes you bolt whenever you feel uneasy."

He rested his hands on his hips. "I didn't say it's when I feel uneasy. It's a defense mechanism. I'm a..."

"Lover, not a fighter?" Crimson arched a brow.

No, he was going to say something else, but the moment the word flitted into his mind, it dissolved like cotton candy in the rain. "This was a mistake. I shouldn't have come here."

"Of course you should." Sophie dropped her arms by her sides. "You've got the most powerful witch in New Orleans *and* an earthbound angel in your corner. They'll help you get your memories back."

Her magic radiated toward him, trying to reach his rabbit and bind it in her metaphorical shackles. He threw up his hands in defense and backed away. "I asked you to stop."

Sophie frowned. "I'm not doing anything."

"Yes, you are." He might not have sensed it

before, but he damn sure did now. The calmness his rabbit felt being near Destiny was honest and real. This thing Sophie had been doing to him since they met was anything but.

He took two more steps backward, the first landing firmly on the wooden porch. The second, however, met air. His ass smacked the railing half a second before his right leg exited solid ground. The impact pitched his upper body forward as the lower half went down. His left knee buckled, and he tumbled, catching himself with his hands on the porch before rolling off and landing in a bed of daffodils.

"Pete!" Destiny rushed down the steps and dropped to her knees beside him. "Oh, goodness. Are you hurt?"

"Ow." He sat up and examined his arm. His sweater had hung up on a nail, the sleeve ripping open from elbow to wrist, but that wasn't the worst of it. His forearm also had a go with the nail, and a massive gash stretched the length of it, blood gushing from the wound.

"Bandages," Destiny shouted to the women on the porch. "We need bandages. And maybe a hospital."

"No." He ripped what was left of his sleeve off and rose to his feet, brushing the dirt from his pants with his uninjured arm. "It'll heal. Shifters heal fast."

"Not that fast." Sophie eyed the wound.

Pete started to wave away her comment, but she was right. The gash stitched itself together in seconds, leaving no scar or redness in its wake. He blinked, turning his arm over and back, the drying blood on his skin the only indication he'd been injured at all.

Logic said he should agree with Sophie, that no shifter could heal that quickly. Something else told him it was completely normal for him. That he'd healed himself in seconds his entire life.

If only he could mend the embarrassment heating his cheeks. Rabbits were supposed to be quick and sure-footed, yet he'd tumbled off the porch like a clumsy panda climbing a swing. And right in front of this copper-haired image of sheer perfection.

Too bad he couldn't tap his foot, open up a rabbit hole, and hop inside. Instead, he shoved his ripped sleeve into his pocket and trudged toward the walk. "I'm going to find the local herd."

"Herd?" Destiny followed him. "Why are you looking for cows?"

He couldn't stop the laugh resonating in his chest as he turned toward her. "Rabbit herd. I need to find shifters like me so I can figure out what happened."

Why the hell was he laughing and grinning from ear to ear? And what was it about this woman that could turn him from being ready to bolt to being perfectly happy rooted to the spot? He wanted to knock himself upside the head and get his mind straight, but as she furrowed her brow, all he could think about was wrapping his arms around her and never letting go. *What is wrong with me?*

"But we know what happened to you," she said. "And I thought a group of rabbits was called a fluffle."

"I like 'flop' myself," Crimson said.

Pete clenched his teeth. "Fluffle is a word that has only been around for a few years, thanks to social media. Herd is the modern English term we use. Flop isn't a thing."

The witch shrugged. "It should be."

"Fluffle is so cute, though." Destiny smiled, making his chest tighten. She could call it a fluffle, a flop, or a fucking fuzz for all he cared.

He shook his head, chasing away the thought. Destiny was there when he first realized he couldn't remember anything. That meant she was there when it happened. She and the vampires had to be responsible. He didn't need to get all warm and fuzzy for the woman who probably fried his brain.

But it seemed he couldn't help himself.

"Fluffle is cute." Sophie leaned on the railing. "It's not very manly though."

He wanted to argue that toxic masculinity wasn't the same as being a man, but what was the point? Once he got his life back, he'd never see these women again. "Thanks for your help."

"But you haven't let us help you," Destiny said.

"You've done enough." His stomach clenched as he uttered the last word, his body and soul insisting he shouldn't walk away from her, but he had to focus on what was left of his mind.

He turned to stride up the walk, but the atmosphere shimmered in front of him. A glowing red line formed in the air, splitting down the center and opening a portal to...was that a restaurant kitchen on the other side?

Before he could get a better look, a man stepped through the hole in reality, and it slammed shut behind him. No, not a man.

A demon. *Fluff me.* The last thing he needed was to add a hellion to this motley mix.

"I'm out." He strode past the gate and made it three steps onto the sidewalk before Destiny clutched his hand, stopping him in his tracks.

"Please, Pete," she said. "That's just Mike."

Angels, vampires, shifters, witches, and now this? Was the entire population of New Orleans made up of supes? "He's a *demon.*"

"Who's in recovery. I promise he's harmless. Just don't make any deals with him." She glanced at their entwined hands and let him go.

He immediately missed the physical contact, which was about the stupidest way for him to feel. He shouldn't trust her, shouldn't give a damn about her, but the way she pleaded with her eyes melted his heart into a puddle right there in his chest.

Crimson walked down the steps and wrapped her arms around the demon, kissing him on the cheek. "You hear that, honey? She says you're harmless."

Mike chuckled. "I try to be. Speaking of harmless demons, is the angel food cake order ready? The Hellions Anonymous meeting is starting soon."

"Shoot. No, it's not, but I'll get it ready. I just..." She flashed Pete that heart-melting, pleading look again. "Will you come back to the bakery with me? I know you don't trust me yet, but there is so much at stake right now, and you're at the center of it. I can't lose you again."

"Lose me..." The appropriate response would've been to say she never had him to begin with, but the words didn't feel right on his tongue. She did have him. *Had* had him all along.

"Please." She took a step toward him. "My cakes help the demons in recovery stay that way. They temper their magic to help them keep control of their urges. It's my purpose in this realm."

His stomach growled in response, and he pressed a hand to his abdomen as if he could silence its protest. When was the last time he'd eaten?

"You must be starving. I can fix you something to eat while I'm working." She started to reach for him, but she clutched her hands over her heart instead.

"Didn't the last thing you fed him cause all the trouble to begin with?" Sophie asked.

"Not helpful," Destiny said through clenched teeth.

Did he eat something at the bakery? His memory of last night was fuzzy at best, but he vaguely remembered a strawberry sauce. Or was it that Destiny's dress reminded him of strawberries?

"How about I whip up some dinner while you're getting the order ready," Mike said. "Pete, you can get cleaned up at Destiny's and y'all can come over to eat when you're done."

"I..." He was starving. There was no denying that, but could he really be stupid enough to trust these people?

Mike swiped a hand through the air, opening another portal. This time, a white house with blue shutters and a sign that read *Sweet Destiny's* stood on the other side. "I can get you home in a jiffy."

"No, thank you." Destiny raised her hands and shook her head adamantly. "Using demon transportation is entirely against the rules. I'll make my own hole."

"Suit yourself." Mike shrugged and closed his portal. "I suppose that's one good thing about Satan. He doesn't care for rules."

Destiny visibly shuddered at the mention of the devil, but she composed herself, straightening her spine and turning toward Pete. "Will you come home with me? If I don't get Mike's order ready, we'll have demons running amuck all over the city."

He took a deep breath and sighed heavily, his

stomach growling once again on cue. It appeared he was, indeed, stupid enough to trust them. "I suppose I could eat."

"Thank you." Her smile rendered him incapable of doing anything but accepting her outstretched hand.

She waved her free arm through the air like Mike had done, but the fabric of reality didn't tear. Her brow furrowed, and she tried again, and a third time. "What in heaven's name?"

"Remember the email?" Crimson asked. "No more magic."

Destiny let out a heavy exhale, dropping his hand and pulling out her phone. "I'll call a ride share." She typed on the screen. "Shoot. It's fifteen minutes away."

"Two steps and you can be home." Mike opened another portal, revealing Destiny's bakery literally two steps away. "The HA meeting starts in half an hour."

Pete eyed the opening. Surely it wasn't against the rules for her to use a simple mode of transportation. If it was, the rule was ridiculous...worthy of being broken. "I vote the fast way. We can't have demons running amuck, can we?" He grinned and winked at Destiny.

She sucked in a quick breath and pressed a hand to her chest as if his simple gesture had a magic of its own. "I can't. It's against the rules."

"Will it hurt you to go through?" If so, he'd never have suggested it. Otherwise...fluff the rules.

"Well, no, but..."

"It's just a shortcut." Sophie descended the steps. "A quick way from one place in this realm to another. I can get started on the order for you if you really need to wait for your ride."

Destiny's phone buzzed, and she frowned at the screen. "The driver canceled. It's searching for another one."

"You know how it is here, Des," Crimson said. "It could be an hour."

"I don't know." Destiny worried her lower lip between her teeth. "Maybe, since it would be for the greater good, I could... I just don't know."

Pete looked at the bakery through the demon's portal. The edges of the tear were bright red when he'd first opened it, but now they were fading, the opening growing smaller. Mike's eyes tightened, the exertion of keeping it open through Destiny's indecisiveness taking an obvious toll.

Honestly, he couldn't see what the problem was. She needed to get home, and her friend had given her a way. It wasn't like she'd have to make a pit stop in Hell before she made it there. Or would she? There was one way to find out.

He stepped through.

"Pete, no! I can't lose you again." Destiny rushed in behind him.

SEVEN

"I can't believe you did that. I can't believe *I* did that." Destiny wrung her hands and stared at the spot where the portal had once hung in the air. She was toast. Burnt toast. "I might as well grind up my wings and make divinity cookies out of them."

Pete's eyes widened in horror. "Is that really how they make them?"

She huffed and shook her head. "Of course not."

"I'm going to prep dinner." Mike started to pat her shoulder but let his hand drop to his side. "Everything is going to be okay."

"Is it?" she asked, though she didn't expect an answer. Mike was a demon, which meant as long as he didn't hurt people, he could do whatever the hell he wanted. And Pete...apparently the man in charge of bringing joy to children all over the world every spring had a rebellious streak. Who would've guessed?

Destiny had no magic, a tick-tocking deadline, and a boss who was ready to slap a pink slip across her face the second she messed up again. How in heaven could everything turn out okay?

"Let me know when the cakes are ready. I'll drop them at the civic center and meet y'all back at my place for dinner." He strolled toward his home, right next door to hers.

Destiny turned to her bakery and found Pete waiting for her at the gate, his hands in his pockets, a sheepish expression on his face. She marched toward him, ready to tell him off, to say he couldn't go hopping into any old hole he came across.

"I get the feeling I've never been fond of rules," he said before she could begin her rant. "I'm sorry."

"You..." His apology disarmed her, so she blew a hard breath through her nose and opened the gate, continuing her march toward the house. "Rules are what keep order in the universe."

She stopped outside the door and whirled

toward him. "It's my job, the sole purpose of my existence, to maintain the balance here in New Orleans. An angel even poking a finger through a demon hole is... Well, it's..."

"What she said?" He grinned.

Her teeth clicked audibly.

He held up his hands. "I apologize. That was crass."

"No kidding." Though the comment did help ease her tension a tiny smidge.

He ascended the front steps. "It's against the rules, and you like to follow them."

"Exactly. I have to." She opened the door, but he caught her hand before she could step inside.

"I have a feeling your job isn't the sole purpose of your existence." His palm was warm, the expression in his eyes sincere.

Her pulse quickened, and she swallowed the dryness from her throat before tugging from his grasp and stepping through the threshold. "Apologies and kind words don't change the fact that you made me use Mike's hole."

At least he had the courtesy to stifle his laugh as he followed her inside. He stopped in the center of the room and turned his head, taking in the scene. "This place is so familiar."

"Because you were just here last night. Come on." She gestured for him to follow her through the kitchen and up the steps, her stomach twisting and turning the whole way up.

"To be fair," he said as he joined her upstairs, "I didn't *make* you do anything. You poked Mike's hole of your own volition, but I am sorry I put you in the position to make that decision."

She tightened her lips and ground her teeth. Pete was right. No one had shoved her through. She could blame him all she wanted, but she'd used Mike's hole...his portal...all on her own. If Gabriela found out what she'd done, she'd surely strip her wings permanently, effective immediately.

So... Destiny would just have to make sure she never found out.

And anyway, what else could the archangels expect? They'd unplugged her from the collective consciousness, stripped her of all magic, and rendered her essentially human while demanding she perform an angelic feat. And then there was Pete...

Her own conundrums aside, she had to find a way to restore his memories. She owed him that much.

"Christ on a cracker." She pressed a hand to her forehead. "This is such a mess."

"I've never seen anything less of a mess in my entire life...or so I assume." Pete turned a circle in the living room. "Neat freak much?"

Destiny followed his gaze to a bookcase filled with her favorite hardcovers, all in their proper places, alphabetized by author and then series and title, as they should be. "Not my house. Me, you, this whole situation is a mess. I don't..." She flung her hands into the air and let them fall to her sides. "It's an absolute hot mess express. How am I supposed to—"

She clamped her mouth shut, lest she mention Easter in front of him again. The last time she tried to convince him he was the Easter Bunny, he'd turned tail and hopped away. If he wanted to pretend he was nothing more than a shifter, she would go along for now. What else could she do?

"Supposed to what?" he asked.

She opened a linen closet and pulled out a fluffy yellow towel. "Why are you here?"

"You promised me a shower and a meal. What man can say no to that?" He rubbed the back of his neck and flashed a lopsided smile that made her pulse race.

"Yesterday, you wanted nothing to do with me, and now you're about to strip naked in my house. Why the sudden trust?" She offered the towel, and he accepted it.

He pressed his lips into a hard line, his gaze seeming to penetrate to her soul. She could practically hear the gears turning in his mind as he contemplated his answer. "I don't know."

She laughed dryly. "I suppose you don't. The bathroom is at the end of the hall. If you'll toss out your clothes, I'll put them in the wash."

He moved toward the bathroom, stopping just inside the door and turning to her. "I don't remember how we met or what caused my amnesia, but honestly? I can't imagine ever wanting nothing to do with you."

He shrugged, the gesture adding *and that's the gods-honest truth* to his statement before he closed the door.

"Heaven, help me." She stood there in the hallway, her lips slightly parted. Or, hell, maybe her mouth hung open like a fish. Her heart flip-flopped in her chest, and the roiling in her stomach turned into flitting butterfly wings.

Why, in the name of the allfather, did that one

simple sentence have the power to burrow deep inside her like this?

It wasn't like he'd confessed his love and utter devotion to her, as if that were even possible. All he'd said was that he couldn't imagine feeling animosity toward her. That didn't mean anything, yet something in her soul insisted it did.

"Thank you." The door cracked open, and Pete dropped a pile of clothes onto the floor before closing and locking it.

See, dummy? He locked the door. He doesn't trust you after all. She scooped up the clothes and carried them to the washing machine. His sweater was ruined, but at least his t-shirt was still in one piece. She dropped the sweater into the machine and pressed his t-shirt to her nose, inhaling deeply.

He had an earthy scent with a hint of sweetness, like fresh-cut grass and jasmine, and she closed her eyes, letting it wrap around her. She swayed on her feet and opened her eyes. *Get a grip, girl.*

She tossed in the shirt and patted his pants pockets, hoping to find a wallet or phone or anything that could prove his identity to him. They were all empty. Did he really leave the fae realm empty-pocketed?

She poured in the detergent and set it to the quick-wash cycle when the doorbell rang.

"Shoot. The cakes." She rushed downstairs and unlocked the front door to let Crimson inside. "I have them in the fridge. I just need to box them up."

"No problem." She followed Destiny through the storefront and into the kitchen. "I brought some of Mike's clothes if he wants to change."

"Thank you." Destiny pulled a tray of mini angel food cakes from the fridge and added two dozen to a box.

"Mike is making his famous eggplant Napoleon." Crimson laid the clothes on the counter and accepted the box. "See you in fifteen?"

"Gods willing." She let her friend out the back door and returned upstairs.

The water shut off, so she padded down the hall and tapped on the door. "Pete? I've got some of Mike's clothes for you to borrow until yours are ready.

The door swung open, and steam wafted into her face, blurring her vision for half a second. She blinked it back into focus, and this time, her mouth really did drop open. She snapped it shut and licked her lips, trying with all her might to keep her gaze on Pete's face.

A lock of wet hair curled onto his forehead, and she tightened her grip on the clothes to stop herself from brushing it into place. She swallowed hard, and her traitorous gaze slid down all six feet of him.

Pecs, abs, a trail of soft hair disappearing into the towel wrapped around his waist. "Yum."

He arched a brow. "Thanks?"

"Oh, dear lord. I don't... I shouldn't have..." She shoved the clothes against his chest and spun away. "I didn't mean to say that." *Not out loud anyway.*

"No worries." He chuckled and clicked the door shut, and Destiny tipped her head toward the ceiling, wishing Gabriela would reach down and yank her into the repository. That file clerk job was looking better and better.

PETE PUT on the borrowed clothes and looked at himself in the mirror. The shirt fit okay, but the pants were too big in the waist. Shame they didn't send over a belt too. He frowned at the sagging khakis, and his skin tingled with an odd magic.

He was used to the tingle that preceded the shift. When his rabbit wanted to take control, his entire body vibrated. This was different.

The tingle gathered in his abdomen, wrapping around to his back. He blinked twice, and suddenly, the pants fit as if they were tailored just for him. *Odd, indeed.*

He must have witch ancestry. There was no other explanation. Then again, witches generally had to cast spells or at least state their intention for their magic to work. His seemed to do its thing whenever it wanted to. Could he have fae blood? He didn't feel anything within him except his rabbit, but it was obvious there was something *other* inside him.

Also obvious was his attraction to the angel waiting outside the doorway. She was beautiful, yes, but what he felt for her ran soul deep. He was there, with her, for a reason. Goddess knew what it was, but he couldn't deny it.

She's mine, his rabbit said in his mind. *She's my mate.*

He sucked in a sharp breath as the word rang in his mind. How could that be? He'd known her all of twenty-four hours...or so he could recall. How could his animal figure out something that life-altering in a single day?

She's the one, his rabbit said again. Was this Fate in action?

Everything happened for a reason, whether he could remember what it was or not. Sometimes the reason was nothing more than making a stupid decision, but it was a reason just the same. He'd done something that led him to the bakery last night. But the catalyst didn't matter, did it? He was there now, and *that* mattered.

He brushed an errant lock of hair from his forehead and opened the door. Destiny wasn't in the hallway, so he padded to the living room and found her perched on the edge of a pastel yellow chair, wringing her hands. Her anxiety was palpable, and he wanted nothing more than to take it away, to shoulder the burden for her.

The feeling was foreign to him, though. Was it because he couldn't remember his past, or was it because he'd never felt such a connection to anyone in his life...because she was his mate?

"What can I do to help?" he asked.

Her jaw worked from side to side, and she pinned him with her blue-eyed gaze. "For starters, you can remember who you are."

He inhaled deeply, holding her gaze until she looked away. She'd decorated her home in soft pastels. Paintings of flowers adorned the light gray walls, and a powder blue rug lay beneath her rose-colored sofa. The space felt welcoming, like home.

He sank onto the sofa adjacent to her chair and rested his hands on his knees. "What if I'm not supposed to remember? What if this is my chance to start over? To live in the moment because there's nothing from my past holding me back. If the gods willed me to lose my—"

She scoffed. "The gods didn't give you amnesia. I did, and if I don't fix it, my life is over."

"You did." His brow furrowed as he tried to recall what had happened. "I remember vampires, but I don't know them. And you were there, but... I feel like you've always been there. I've always known you, haven't I? We're..."

"No." She shook her head. "We met for the first time last night. The gods didn't will this on you, believe me. I stupidly left a magical cake on the counter, you ate it, and it wiped your memory. You ran away before I could even attempt to help you, and now my magic has been stripped, but that doesn't matter because I have no clue how to reverse what I've done."

"Why...?" His mind spun with so many questions. Why was he there? Why did he eat a cake that wasn't his? Why was her magic stripped?

If his rabbit was so certain of it, why did she not recognize him as her mate?

"You came to my bakery to meet Gaston. You do know him, from a long, long time ago. You needed his help with something. Do you remember what it was?"

There was that pleading look again, melting his heart even more. He closed his eyes, willing his brain to give him a shred of something, anything that would make her happy. "I've got nothing."

"And I've only got two weeks to help you remember everything before I become human for good."

"Why will you become human?"

She shook her head. "Performing miracles is the other aspect of my job in this realm, but it takes months to get them approved. Becoming human is my punishment if I don't make it happen in the next two weeks, but this is a long story that we don't have time for. We need to focus on getting your memories back."

"Can you not ask your boss for help? Escalate it to a manager?"

She laughed dryly. "I tried. My boss is out to get me."

"Maybe go over her head?"

"My boss's boss is out to get me too. Angels aren't supposed to make mistakes, and on the rare —or not so rare in my case—occasion that they do, they…I…have to fix it myself. Everything magical an angel can do is for the greater good or the good of the receiver, but I somehow manage to screw things up anyway."

He drummed his fingers on his knees, a sense of resolve—of acceptance—settling in his chest. "There you go. You gave me amnesia for my own good."

"Well, it sure as sugar isn't for the greater good," she mumbled.

"How do you know?"

"I just do."

He nodded, scooting to the edge of his seat. "Can I tell you what I know?"

"That won't take long." She leaned her head back and closed her eyes. "I'm sorry. That was rude and not very angelic of me."

"It's okay. You're stressed. I feel like I have that effect on people." Why, he had no clue, but he was as certain as the fluff on his butt that he—or the way he acted—caused stress in other people's lives, Destiny's included.

She lifted her head from the chair and turned to him. "Tell me what you know."

Mate, his rabbit said again in his mind. *I get it, buddy, and I believe you. I feel it too.* His throat thickened, a lump forming just above his Adam's apple, and he swallowed hard. Destiny wasn't a shifter, so he had to do this with finesse. To make her see they were meant to be without pushing her away. "I know you're not as much of a mess as you claim to be."

She laughed, but he held up a hand.

"I know you feel the need to be perfect."

"I have to. It's in my job description."

"Then maybe you don't have the right job. Perfection sounds about as fun as cleaning sand from your butt cheeks, and this so-called Hot Mess Express..." He gestured to her. "I find her intriguing. I believe...I *know* I'm here with you for a reason. I know Destiny isn't just your name. It's what you are to me. You, Destiny, are my destiny."

"Well, I..." She clamped her mouth shut and tilted her head. "Don't be silly. I promise you've only known me for a day."

"Then a day is all I needed. You're supposed to be in my life. Shifters always know when..." The look of unease on her face stopped him from finishing, and he shrugged, attempting to downplay his words. "Or maybe that's the amnesia talking."

So much for finesse. He'd gone too far. The soul-deep connection he felt with her wasn't reciprocated yet, and he should have sensed that.

She held his gaze for a beat or two before rising to her feet. "We shouldn't keep Crimson and Mike waiting. Let's go eat."

Mate, his rabbit insisted. *You have to be patient, buddy. Winning her heart is going to take some time.*

EIGHT

oly hellhounds in heaven. The cake Pete ate must've short-circuited his sense of judgment when it wiped his memory. How else could you explain his crazy idea that she was his destiny? It might have been her name, but she was absolutely nothing of the sort. She'd made his already bad situation worse. Nothing more. Nothing less.

Him meeting her was the exact opposite of destiny. It was a curse.

She pulled her sweater tight against her chest as they trekked across the yard to Mike and Crimson's house. The chilly March wind stung her cheeks, and her eyes watered as she knocked on the back door.

Sophie opened it. "Hey, y'all. Come on in. There

was a famine demon on the verge of wiping out a grocery store, so Mike stayed at the HA meeting to talk him down. Crimson is finishing the food."

"Should I send over more cakes?" Destiny spun and swung her arm to gesture at her bakery, but the back of her hand smacked Pete's nose, making a painful cracking sound.

"Ow." His eyes watered, and he pressed his hands to his face, popping his nose back into place.

"I'm so sorry. Are you okay?" She rested a hand on his shoulder. See? The Hot Mess Express had to be a curse on the poor, unsuspecting Easter Bunny. She'd given him amnesia, made him a little cuckoo, and now she'd broken his nose. What was next?

He squeezed his eyes shut before opening them wide and gripping her hand, sandwiching it between both of his. "I'm fine. Shifters are fast healers. See?" He wiggled his nose in an adorable way that only a rabbit could.

She nodded and tugged from his grasp, scurrying inside to avoid feeling any more warm fuzzies for the man.

Like her bakery, Mike's restaurant occupied the bottom floor of his building, so they took the staircase up to the living area where Crimson stood in the kitchen, putting the finishing touches on their dinner.

"Do you prefer shrimp or crawfish with your eggplant?" she asked.

He scrunched his brow and rubbed his thumb on his chin. "Neither? I'm pretty sure I'm a vegetarian."

Crimson set the plate of fried shellfish on the counter. "No problem. Destiny is too."

"I'll take both," Sophie said. "I'm ravenous."

Crimson laughed. "Ever since you got your wolf, you've chowed down like a gluttony demon at an all-you-can-eat buffet."

"Gotta feed my beast." She popped a shrimp into her mouth. "Mmm. My compliments to the chef."

"Have a seat." Crimson carried two glasses of sweet tea to the table, and Sophie followed with another two.

Pete pulled out a chair and flashed his jewel-green gaze at Destiny. She waited for him to sit down, but he just stood there, holding the back of the seat.

"Let the man be chivalrous," Sophie said around

another mouthful of shrimp. "Sit." She gave Destiny's hip a shove.

Pete smiled, and she accepted the gesture, sitting just as he slid the chair forward and tucked her into the seat. He sat catty-corner to her, and Crimson set the plates on the table before joining them.

The savory scents of thyme and garlic filled her senses, making her mouth water. Fried eggplant slices sandwiched roasted tomatoes with melted mozzarella, and a side of pasta with marinara complemented the recipe perfectly.

She took a bite, closing her eyes as the flavors danced and melded on her tongue. "This is delicious."

"Very." Pete's knee brushed hers beneath the small table, and she pulled away.

Jane hadn't been kidding when she'd said the attraction between them was off-the-charts hot. If he were any old rabbit shifter, she might entertain the idea of meant to be...or let him hop on down her bunny trail at the very least.

But he was the frigging Easter Bunny for heaven's sake. He might as well have been the allfather because, either way, there was no chance in all the realms that he and she were meant to be anything more than a walking curse and her victim.

"So…" Sophie set her fork down. "Now that you've found him, what are you going to do with him?"

Destiny's stomach fluttered. She could think of a few things she'd like to do. "Umm…" She cleared her throat. "I have to figure out a way to give him his memory back. I'm hoping Crimson might know a spell to help."

"Already on it," Crimson said. "I've got something that might just do the trick."

"Then what?" Sophie took a sip of tea, eyeing Destiny over the rim of the glass.

"Then, we…" She cut her gaze to Pete as he took his last bite of eggplant. "Save Easter."

He coughed. Then he sucked in a massive breath and wheezed. His eyes bulged, his mouth hanging open as he slapped at his throat. Oh, dear lord, he was choking. Why had Destiny tempted Fate by asking what was next?

"You okay, Pete?" Crimson slapped his back. His body heaved as if he were going to cough it out, but not even the tiniest bit of breath made it past the wad of eggplant lodged in his throat.

His face turned red from straining. As the hue

morphed to purple, Destiny leaped to her feet and moved behind him, fisting one hand below his ribcage, bracing it with the other, and jerking inward and up. He made an *uh* sound with her second thrust, and with her third, the eggplant dislodged from his throat and shot across the table, splatting right in the center of Sophie's forehead.

It slid down, leaving a trail of mush and spit before hitting her nose and plopping onto her plate.

Pete heaved in a breath, pressing his hand to his chest and gripping the edge of the table.

"Are you okay?" Still standing behind him, Destiny wrapped her arms around his shoulders, her left cheek resting against his right.

He pressed a hand to the side of her head, gently holding her against him. "I'm good. Thank you for saving my life."

She scoffed and pulled away, returning to her seat. "You might've passed out, but I definitely did not save your life. You're an immortal fae. You can't die."

"I'm fine too. Thanks for asking." Sophie wiped a napkin across her forehead.

Pete took a giant gulp of tea and folded his hands on the table. "My rabbit is just a rabbit. I can't be the Easter Bunny. That's something I wouldn't forget."

"Then you don't know how strong angel magic can be," Crimson said. "I was raised by angels. Their magic is stickier than glitter in a drag queen's cleavage."

"I'm just a rabbit shifter," he muttered, sounding more like he was trying to convince himself of the fact as he rose and carried his plate to the sink.

Destiny followed, joining him as he rinsed his dishes and put them in the dishwasher. "You are a rabbit shifter, but you're also a fae."

"Wouldn't I feel it if I were?" He dried his hands on a towel and leaned against the counter.

She paused, eyeing him, looking for signs he might be ready to shift and tuck tail. His calm demeanor and the casual way he leaned gave her the courage to push further. "You don't feel it because your fae side is the part my magical cake subdued."

He screwed his mouth to one side. "I suppose the demons forget they're creatures from hell when they eat them as well?"

"Well, no, but..."

"They don't because the magic she uses is

tailored for demons." Crimson took the plate from Destiny's hand. "She spent years perfecting the spell to subdue their urges without turning them into zombified hellions. It was never meant for a fae or a shifter or anyone else to consume."

He straightened, a shadow of unease falling across his features. "Since when do angels cast spells?"

"We don't." Destiny clasped her hands. "We don't call it spells."

"Sorry. Witch talk." Crimson added more plates to the dishwasher. "She perfected her angel magic recipe specifically to subdue demons. Now we know it gives faeries amnesia."

"Okay, but that doesn't prove I'm the Easter Bunny." Pete shrugged. "Has a shifter ever eaten one? Maybe it gives anyone who isn't a demon amnesia."

"I suppose that's possible," Crimson said. "Hey Soph, do you want to try one and see what happens? For posterity's sake?"

"Hell, no." Sophie dropped her napkin onto her plate and carried it into the kitchen. "I love my life. Satan's balls will rot and fall off before I'll chance forgetting everything that's made me who I am."

"No, no." Destiny shook her head, her posture

sinking. "No one else needs to get involved. I already can't fix what I've broken."

"Hey." Pete stepped toward her and lightly gripped her shoulders, ducking his head to catch her gaze. "I might not remember my past, but I'm not broken."

"I am." She lifted her head. Even her closest friends wouldn't take a chance on her magic. Maybe now he'd rethink that meant-to-be feeling he had about her.

"Your powers are bound," Sophie said. "There's a difference."

"We need to focus." Destiny shook out her hands before pressing her palms together. "Demons have to eat the cakes every week because the magic wears off. Pete, do you feel it wearing off? Are any memories returning? Anything at all?"

He lifted his gaze upward and to the right, tilting his head as he thought. "Nothing before I left the bakery last night."

"You don't remember asking Gaston for help with the hens?" She pressed her fingers to her temples. "You came to New Orleans to see Gaston because a vampire drained half a dozen Easter hens. Because you're the Easter Bunny and you need to save your holiday."

He dropped his arms and returned to his chair. "There's just no way."

"Hold on." Sophie drummed her fingers on the table. "What about the coven door? You used magic to unlock it. Regular shifters can't do that."

Destiny gasped. "And your clothes. If you were just a shifter, your clothes would have fallen off when your rabbit came through. But they didn't, did they?"

He opened his mouth as if to deny it, but he closed it again, looking thoughtful for a moment. "I was thinking I could be part witch. I suppose fae is a possibility too, but I just feel like that's something I would know. The fae are from an entirely different realm, and I feel grounded here."

"I've got a spell that might help you." Crimson set a copper bowl on the counter and took three herb jars from the cabinet. "Lie on the couch, and I'll fix you right up."

***

PETE EYED the sofa and debated the situation in his mind. Destiny's magic was the cause of his amnesia. That much he believed. And they were right about the extra powers he could tap into, however unwittingly he did it. Being part fae was the only thing that truly made sense.

The women stood in the kitchen as Crimson worked on the spell. He caught a glimpse of Destiny's copper hair as she walked past the counter, and his stomach tightened. His rabbit insisted he allow the witch to perform her ritual on him for the sole fact that it would please his mate.

His mate. Heat spread through his chest at the thought, but he forced his emotions down. Now was not the time for mate talk. He turned a circle in the living room, admiring the paintings adorning the walls. Detailed still-life and swamp scenes occupied the far wall, while colorful cityscapes decorated the adjacent one. He stepped toward a portrait of a man sitting on a red throne hanging above the television.

"Is that Mike?" he asked.

"It sure is," Crimson said from behind him.

"Is he a prince?"

"Nope." She laughed. "I channel the goddess Morrigan when I paint, and that one is... Well, it's a long story. Maybe I'll tell you sometime."

"She's talented, isn't she?" Destiny asked. "Does the art jog any memories? You're an artist yourself."

He liked the paintings and could tell they were

done well. They stirred a feeling inside him he couldn't identify, but as for recalling memories... "No, nothing."

"Come lie down and let Crimson do her thing." Destiny sank onto the arm of the sofa. "She won't hurt you like I did."

His legs carried him to the couch before his mind could catch up with the movement. Hell, every part of him except his mind was completely on board with all of this. "You didn't hurt me."

"I just made you forget your entire identity."

He sank onto a cushion. "Maybe that was meant to be."

She laughed. "Sure. You were meant to forget everything, and I was meant to... Let's try the spell."

He lay back, resting his head on a cushion and looking up at her. "Promise I won't forget the last two days? I'm enjoying getting to know you."

A ghost of a smile crossed her lips before she frowned. "Honestly, I have no idea how it will affect you."

"I'll give it a whirl, anyway." Because he would do everything in his power to make her happy. His rabbit insisted.

"It might make you dizzy," Crimson said. "I did this spell to help a bull shifter unlock a repressed memory, and he passed out an hour later in his China shop. He broke a bunch of dishes and slept for twelve hours straight. His wife was not pleased."

She lit a pink candle on the end table and carried a small bowl toward him before dipping her thumb into the potion and dragging the paste across his forehead. A warming sensation spread upward to his scalp, and he closed his eyes, willing the magic to seep into his brain.

"The spell I'm about to cast works on shifters and witches, so I'm hoping your rabbit side can do the heavy lifting here. Fae are a whole other animal. Witch magic can't touch them, but if we can get your rabbit to remember, then maybe…"

"Let's do it."

She swiped another glob of potion onto his forehead. "The past unlocked. Memories freed. In the name of the goddess, so mote it be."

He waited, keeping his eyes closed tightly as his skin tingled with the witch's magic. He took a deep breath and let it out slowly, but still, he felt nothing but the pricking sensation on his skin.

"Clear your mind," Crimson said.

"That shouldn't be hard," Sophie said before she snorted, making him laugh.

"Not helpful." Destiny's voice was strained. She took things way too seriously.

Pete cleared his throat and focused as Crimson recited the incantation again. He sensed her hands hovering above his head, but still, nothing happened.

On the third recitation, Destiny rested her hand on his forehead. He knew it was her because his entire body responded to her touch, and his rabbit thumped with joy. His muscles relaxed, his thoughts turning to dust bunnies floating on a breeze.

"That's all I've got." Crimson's voice sounded a million miles away. "Pete, did it work?"

He blinked his eyes open, and Destiny removed her hand. "Anything?" she asked.

He sat up and rested his feet on the floor, bringing all his senses back to the present. He searched his mind, sifting through the nothingness, searching for a memory of anything that happened before he ate the enchanted cake.

"Nothing."

"Well, crap." Destiny offered him a towel and pressed the heels of her hands against her brow. "I don't know what else to do."

His heart wrenched at the sight of her pain. He

turned, angling toward her and wiping the potion from his head before taking her hand in his. He opened his mouth to console her, but the energy in the room shifted.

A familiar vibration gathered in the space in front of them, and Destiny shot to her feet before backing into the wall. "Oh, dear. Incoming."

"A goddess." Crimson pressed her hands to her chest. "It's not Morrigan."

"Holy fuck," Sophie said.

A wave of pastel pinks, blues, and yellows shimmered in Crimson's living room. Pete stood and instinctively bowed his head. He'd felt this energy before. He couldn't remember when or where, but his soul knew she was someone he revered.

The light sparkled silver, making his vision turn to a haze as the goddess formed in front of him. He blinked it into focus and took in the ethereal vision before him. Long, rose gold hair. Lavender eyes. A crown of daisies.

He knew this goddess. At least, he thought he did.

"Eostre," Crimson said in reverence. "Welcome to my home."

"Thank you, dear," the goddess said before turning her gaze to him. "Pete, you've been a hard one to find. If not for this witch invoking Morrigan, I'd still be searching."

"Searching?" He tilted his head. "But you're not Morrigan."

"Of course I'm not. She notified me the second she sensed the subject of your friend's spell." She gave him a quizzical look. "Are you okay? Did your vampire friend agree to help us?"

"Umm..." He looked at Destiny, who widened her eyes and lifted her hands in an *I don't know* gesture.

Eostre took his hand, clasping it between both of hers, her brow furrowing as she seemed to read his energy. She stepped back, dropping his hand, her lips parting in a look of unease. She searched his eyes before her gaze wandered over his face. "Something has changed."

"I'm sorry, ma'am," Destiny said, and the goddess snapped her gaze toward her.

A series of emotions flashed across Eostre's face too quickly for him to identify. "It's you." Her eyes wide, she brought a trembling hand toward her face, resting her fingertips against her lips. "Loki's lacy panties. Can it really be?"

"It was an accident." Destiny held her hands up in surrender. "I didn't mean for him to—"

"It's not her fault." He stepped between the goddess and his angel. *His* angel. He liked the sound of that. "Whatever you're here to accuse her of, she didn't do it. She wouldn't hurt a flea."

"Destiny is awry," Eostre whispered.

They all stood in silence for a moment. Destiny stepped out from behind him, but he stayed close by her side, instinct telling him to protect her at all costs. But protect her from what? Eostre was the goddess of spring. What beef could she possibly have with an earthbound angel?

"Do you believe us now, Pete?" Sophie asked.

Eostre closed her eyes for a long blink before squaring her gaze on Sophie. "What does he not believe? I need to know what's going on imme-diately."

Destiny cleared her throat. "He's forgotten he's the Easter Bunny, and it's my fault."

"Forget the past." Eostre turned to him. "It's just as I feared."

NINE

"You are, indeed, the Easter Bunny." Eostre sat at the table across from them, and Destiny took a deep breath to slow her racing heart.

She'd never met an actual goddess before, but the stories of their celestial beauty and commanding presence barely nicked the surface of a description. To say she was in awe would be a massive understatement.

Yes, Destiny was an angel and ethereal herself. She had her own otherworldly beauty and calming presence that awed the people in this realm. Big deal. Eostre was way further up the hierarchy than any earthbound angel, and she reigned in a different pantheon. As Crimson said before, the fae were an entirely different animal.

"You have to believe me now. Why else would a goddess be here?" Destiny rested her hand atop Pete's, and he immediately turned his over, lacing his fingers through hers. Warmth expanded in her chest with his touch, and she didn't know whether to yank her hand away or hold him tighter.

"And you have to believe what you did to him was meant to happen." Eostre's gaze drifted to their entwined hands. "However inconvenient it may be."

Destiny pulled from his grasp. "I've done nothing but screw things up from the moment I met him."

"Exactly," the goddess said. "There is a prophecy in our realm, and it's coming to fruition. You're as much a part of it as Pete and I are."

"That's impossible." She wiped her sweaty palms on her dress.

"This is what Frigg told me." Eostre rested her hands on the table. "'Balance dies when birds lie. Forget the past. Destiny is awry. An act of hubris is all it takes to bring about the end of days. A goddess, nay, her right-hand man will leave this land to devise a plan. A...'" She cleared her throat. "As Fate has willed it, so mote it be."

Eostre paused, her gaze flicking from Destiny to Pete and back again. "She didn't mean destiny in general. She meant you."

Destiny blinked the dryness from her eyes and stared straight ahead. How in heaven's name could a faery prophecy include an angel? Unless she was meant to destroy their oligarchy so the angels could finally claim their realm, it was simply... "Impossible."

"Not really," Sophie said. "Birds *lie* on the ground when they die. I assume that goes for your chickens as well, right?"

"Indeed," Eostre said. "And three more have since been attacked."

"But they're *fae* hens," Destiny said. "The fae are immortal, so they can't—"

"They're only immortal to a certain extent." Eostre looked at Pete, who sat silently, chewing the inside of his cheek. "Unless a fae has been blessed by a goddess..." She glanced at him again. "They are subject to similar laws of life as the vampires in your realm. Aside from sunlight, a fae can be killed by beheading, piercing the heart with iron, and draining of blood."

"This is..." She wanted to say crazy, that the idea of her being part of a fae prophecy was totally bonkers. But Pete thought it ludicrous to say he was the Easter Bunny. If she wanted him to believe, she would have to dive halo first into the insanity too.

Eostre looked at Destiny, her brow pinching, a strange countenance falling across her features. Was it sadness, or maybe longing? She couldn't decipher the goddess's expression, but it made her want to squirm in her seat, so she looked away.

"Pete, do you remember speaking with your vampire friend?" Eostre folded her hands on the table.

He flattened his. "Vaguely. Two vampires were in Destiny's bakery when...when it happened." He waved a hand by his head. "But I don't remember what we talked about."

"Is it dark out yet?" Eostre turned to Crimson, who'd been sitting silently on a stool at the kitchen counter. "I need to speak with the vampire."

"Just about. I'll call Gaston." She rose and strode into the bedroom.

The goddess stood and pushed her chair beneath the table. "I must take Pete home. I have already added disruption to the balance by meeting with you."

Destiny knew all about the importance of balance, but the idea of Pete going "home" sat in her gut like a brick of two-week-old meatloaf. Why she felt so strongly about it, she couldn't say, but she knew, deep in her heart, she didn't want him to leave.

"I am home," he said, and her breath caught.

Eostre smiled sadly. "I need you, Peter. Easter *must* happen. Our entire pantheon is at stake."

"Bad news," Crimson said as she returned to the kitchen. "I couldn't get ahold of Gaston or Jane, so I called his wife, Maeve. The Magistrate sequestered the council members and their advisors to work out some kind of something or other. They'll be out of pocket for the next two nights."

"Did he tell Maeve anything else?" Eostre asked.

"Just what you already know about the hens." She sank onto a stool.

"Come, Pete." The goddess took his hand, tugging him to his feet. He followed her to the middle of the room, a look of confusion crumpling his brow.

"I don't want to go. I belong here." He looked at Destiny. "With her."

"We'll discuss it later. There's simply no time to spare." Eostre nodded at Destiny, and silver sparkles gathered around her. Her body turned translucent as she prepared to make the jump from the earthly realm to her own, but Pete remained solid. She tugged his hand, attempting to pull him into the magic, but he didn't budge.

"Loki on a lemur, you have got to be kidding." Eostre stopped sparkling and fully returned to the room. She dropped Pete's hand and pressed her palms together, closing her eyes and tapping into her form of the collective consciousness. Or so Destiny assumed.

Funny how they came from different realms, different pantheons, yet their methods were so similar. Being the goddess of spring, Eostre was probably on the same level as Michelle in the angelic hierarchy. Maybe even higher. She could've been conversing with the allfather himself, right there in Crimson's living room.

"I've disrupted the balance too much." Eostre opened her eyes and parked her hands on her hips. "I can't take you home until you remember how to get there yourself."

Crimson arched a brow. "Your leaders won't let you take him home, even though the prophecy talks about the end of days?"

"It's not about *letting* me bring him home. I physically can't. This is all part of Fate's plan." The goddess waved a hand, gesturing to...well, to everything.

The end of days? Destiny's heart sank. In her attempt to convince herself the prophecy couldn't possibly include her, she hadn't paid close enough attention to the words. The end of days meant the end of the world in faery speak. Did she really bring *that* to their doorstep?

No, she couldn't let it happen.

"I know angels and fae gods aren't supposed to interact, but honestly, I'm a nobody." She stood and clasped her hands. "My boss bound my magic because of all my screwups, so I'm basically human. Surely your higher ups will see that and let you..."

Eostre shook her head. "Destiny, my child, you must restore his memory."

"I would if I could, but I'm magicless."

"Then you have to find another way." She crossed her arms over her chest, holding herself as if she were afraid she might fall to pieces.

"I have a question," Sophie said, raising her hand. "Can't you fix his memory? I mean, you're a goddess and all."

"I'm afraid not. Fae magic, even that of a goddess, cannot undo what an angel has done. Not when Fate has willed it to happen." She straightened her spine, giving Destiny a pointed look.

"Helga, the golden goose, has offered help with the eggs," Eostre said. "Her flock will provide enough this year, but Pete must be the one to deliver them. He can't do that until you undo the bind you've put on him."

A lump the size of a goose egg formed in Destiny's throat. She tried to swallow it, but she couldn't force it down. "I don't know how," she whispered.

"Can't someone else deliver them this year?" Sophie asked. "Surely Pete has helpers. Or what about Santa? Maybe he can do it."

Destiny shook her head. "Santa wouldn't hide the eggs. He'd just leave them beneath a tree."

"That's no fun." Sophie tapped a finger against her jaw. "The tooth faery?"

"The eggs would get squished beneath the kids' pillows," Crimson said.

Sophie shrugged. "I'm just spitballing here. Help me out."

"It must be Pete." The goddess crossed her arms, shifting her weight to one leg. "He is the *elfen* I chose, and I granted him this power. My life is tied to his, and they are both at stake."

"It'll be okay." He rested a hand on her shoulder. "We'll figure something out."

Destiny held her breath, waiting for his memories to come flooding back. No one in any realm would assume themselves so familiar with a goddess that they could touch her. Yet Pete did so as if he'd known her for millennia.

Which he probably had.

Eostre placed her hand on his. "Do you truly not remember me at all, *mijn elfen*?"

He blinked, his brow furrowing as if her words had knocked loose a shred of memory before he tugged from her grasp. "Why are our lives at stake?"

"If the Easter celebrations fail to happen, you will lose everything." Sympathy rounded her eyes. "No more human or rabbit form. You'll become a mortal robin."

He nodded, his mouth tightening. "And you?"

"I'll be cast out of the realm, and..." She looked at Destiny. "If I no longer hold my seat in the pantheon, the balance will shift."

"And bring about the end of days...thanks to an angel's mistake." Destiny pressed a hand to her chest. "Did I just start a war?"

"I have already said too much and been here too long. Pete must deliver the eggs on Easter morning."

Silver sparkles gathered around her. "Together is the only way you can make it happen."

The goddess disappeared, the glitter fading until no remnants of her presence remained.

Heat crept from Destiny's chest to her neck before spreading across her face and making her ears burn. She truly had committed the flub to end all flubs. Forget her own immortality. That paled in comparison to the consequences Pete and Eostre... the entire fae realm...would face. She'd written them death sentences.

"Destiny." Pete strode toward her, his arms extended like he wanted to hug her, and for half a second, she considered letting him.

But she didn't deserve his sympathy.

She held up her hands to stop him, and tears gathered on her lower lids, her throat thickening until she could barely force out the words, "I have to go. I'll figure out a way to fix this if it kills me."

She darted toward the staircase and stopped on the first step. "Thank you for dinner and for trying to help," she muttered before racing down and returning to her home.

TEN

Pete stood in Crimson's kitchen, staring at the empty doorway. Whew, that was a lot to unpack. A goddess had traveled to the earthly realm to talk to *him*. And then Destiny... How could...? Why would...?

He blew out a hard breath and shook his head. "Fluff if I know."

"Running away seems to be a common theme with y'all." Sophie laughed and brushed her hair behind her shoulder. "Should we follow her?"

"No." Crimson rested her fingertips on the counter. "I recognized the look of mortification on her face. She's embarrassed. We need to let her wallow for a bit before we figure out what to do."

Let her wallow? No, he couldn't do that. He couldn't stand by while she suffered from embarrassment, pain, or even dysentery. His rabbit wouldn't allow it, and neither would the man. "I'll go talk to her."

He started toward the stairs, but Crimson grasped his arm. "Be gentle. She's a perfectionist, so I imagine she's raking herself over the coals."

Gentle. He couldn't think of any other way to be. "Thank you. I'm sure we'll be in touch."

He descended the stairs and hurried across the yard to Destiny's. The back door was locked, but a quick brush of his fingers opened it with ease. Darkness engulfed the bottom floor, so he went up to the living area and found her sitting on the sofa, cradling her head in her hands. He padded toward her and sank onto the cushion next to her.

A sob racked her body, and she sucked in a shaky breath. "You should hate me."

He rubbed her back. "I don't."

"I wouldn't blame you if you did. Eostre too." She rocked back and forth.

"I could never hate you."

She lifted her head and turned toward him, the tear stains on her cheeks making his heart wrench. "You don't know that. You hardly know me at all."

"Tell that to my soul."

She started to look away, but he caught her cheek in his palm. "Ask your soul if it really believes that. We're connected. You must feel it too."

Her lower lip trembled, and she swallowed hard. "This prophecy, this... I don't think..."

"Then *don't* think. Just feel." He grasped both her hands. "I have a feeling you sensed it the moment you met me. We both did." They must have. Sure, he'd freaked and bolted, but the sudden amnesia would make anyone in a situation like that bounce. Truth be told, it wasn't her he'd run from.

"I felt...I feel..." She took a deep breath. "I'm attracted to you, but this...you and me...can't be. In a couple of weeks, I'll be human and you'll be *a bird*. A regular, non-verbal, no-human-side bird. You won't feel anything for me."

He squeezed her hands. "That's not going to happen. I won't let it."

"Of course it is. You heard what Eostre said. I'm awry. I've brought about the end of days because I'm a fuckup. I always have been."

"Don't say that. Words and thoughts are energy. When you say negative things..."

"I draw negative energy toward me. Believe me, I know. That's Angel 101." She tugged from his grasp and wrung her hands in her lap. "I know all the rules. I try to follow them to the letter, but no matter what I do, what job the higher ups have assigned to me, I flub and someone gets hurt. I thought this assignment was the one I could do forever. Live on Earth with the supes and humans. Bake cakes for demons. I thought it would be easy peasy."

She huffed a sardonic laugh. "Holy horns and halos, was I ever wrong. I gave the Easter Bunny amnesia."

"That wasn't your fault." Why did she feel as if she were responsible for the entire world? A wallaby could catch a cold in Australia, and Destiny would find a way to blame herself. "And anyway, Eostre said it happened for a—"

"*Everything* happens for a reason. I know that too." She rolled her eyes and shot to her feet. "I used to be a guardian angel. I had the highest ranking, most coveted job a standard angel could have in all the realms. Did you know that?"

He opened his mouth to answer, but she cut him off.

"No, of course you didn't. No one knows." She paced to her bookcase and rested her hands on a shelf. "I've never told a soul because I failed so miserably in that job."

He shifted his weight on the sofa, angling toward her. "What happened? If you don't mind my asking."

"What do you think?" She laughed dryly. "I had twelve charges like every guardian when they first start out. I was supposed to watch over them, guide their decisions, and keep them safe. Again... Angel 101."

"That's a lot of people to be responsible for."

"It's not, though." She strode to a chair and sank onto the arm. "Others had twenty, thirty. The elite could manage fifty or more."

"Still..." Twelve seemed like a lot to him. Hell, he couldn't imagine being responsible for anyone but himself.

"I lost one. A mother of two died of an opium overdose because I was too busy with another charge to step in and stop her. Her children were sent to a workhouse, and they..." She pressed her lips together and frowned.

"I can imagine that must feel awful, but people die every day. Surely every angel in the realm doesn't take responsibility for each human death. That would be devastating."

She shook her head. "I should have stopped her. Opium was so unpredictable back then, and she'd gotten ahold of a really strong batch. If I'd been there, I could have warned her."

"You were helping another charge."

She scoffed. "I wasn't helping him. I was *with* him. Guardians can appear to their charges as humans when they need a friend or even a random stranger to give them advice. I *appeared* to Jonathan as someone to court."

He scooted down the couch toward her. "Then, I'm sure that's what he needed at the time."

"I'm not, and neither is Gabriela. She yanked me out of that position so fast, my halo nearly slipped off. I was reassigned to holy water distribution, but I fell into the vat we were blessing and pulled two other angels in with me. You can't fly with wet wings, so we were stuck there all night until someone on the next shift found us."

"Sometimes it takes a while to find our calling."

She arched a brow. "It happened three times. After the third, my boss was ready to send me to the repository to be a file clerk, but Michelle, my boss's boss, took pity on me. She sent me here to bake cakes for the demons of New Orleans."

"And this is where you're meant to be." He couldn't say why or how he knew, but he felt it all the way to his bones.

She rose again. "I thought so. I've been here over a century, and I've perfected the recipe to subdue demon magic without harming the hellions. I visited the angelic realm around one hundred fifty years ago to tell Gabriela in person. She acted like it was nothing."

Her shoulders slumped. "Like I was nothing."

Pete stood and stepped toward her, lifting her lowered head with his finger beneath her chin. "You are not nothing. Your role in this realm is important, but your job isn't your identity."

She looked into his eyes, tears gathering on her lower lids before one rolled down her cheek. "Says the literal Easter Bunny."

He smiled softly and wiped it away with his thumb. "Even with that very large piece of me missing from my mind, I'm still here. I think I'm still me. If I never remember my past, I'm okay with that."

He *was* okay with it, anyway. Before Eostre appeared and warned him his life was on the line, he'd have been happy to stay put and spend the rest of his days with Destiny, whether she was "awry" or simply beautifully imperfect.

Now that he knew he was a pawn in a fae prophecy, of course he'd have to act. He couldn't sit by while an entire realm fell apart, but right now, Destiny needed him more.

Another tear rolled down her face, and he wiped it away. His entire being ached at her sadness, and he wanted nothing more than to wrap his arms around her and take it all away. To make her happy. To make her his own.

"I like being here in New Orleans with you." And that really was the gods' honest truth.

"I like you being here too. I just..." She laughed and shook her head. "Would you listen to me? I didn't mean to drag you into my pity party. I'm done now."

"I don't mind. Pity party, dance party, you can invite me to them all." He brushed a lock of hair from her face, tucking it behind her ear. "I want to be here for you."

Her gaze dipped to his mouth, and she slipped out her tongue, moistening her lips before smiling softly. "That's kind of you." She rested her fingertips lightly against his chest.

Her touch made his head spin, and desire

unfurled inside him. *She's mine,* his rabbit said in his mind, and goddess have mercy, did he ever need to make it so. He drifted closer, cupping her cheek in his hand, and her lips parted slightly as she lifted her gaze to meet his.

Heart thumping, he leaned in, his mouth scant centimeters from hers. He waited, giving her ample time to pull away, the anticipation of tasting this sweet angel's lips tightening his core and making his stomach loop.

She didn't pull away. In fact, she leaned in closer, sliding her arms around his waist and pressing her soft, velvety lips to his.

Every muscle in his body seemed to melt as he pulled her to his chest and kissed her. She tasted as sweet as he imagined, like vanilla and lavender. He wasn't sure if it was because of the cakes she baked or because she was an angel, but it didn't matter.

His rabbit leaped with joy, and he drank her in. Her soft curves pressing against him turned his head into a carousel, the sensation both exhilarating and nauseating at the same time, and as he dipped his tongue into her mouth to tangle with hers, he gripped her shoulders to steady himself.

She broke the kiss, pulling back to look at him, and a dark vignette formed around his vision. "Pete?

Are you okay?" She held his face in her hands, and his knees buckled beneath him.

He pitched forward, the vignette closing in, turning into a black tunnel as they tumbled onto the couch. He fell on top of her, and everything went dark.

CHAPTER

ELEVEN

Destiny leaned against the kitchen counter, warming her hands with a mug of coffee and watching the softest, silkiest bunny she'd ever seen sleep on the couch. Holy fluff. Crimson wasn't kidding about the side effects of that spell.

After they'd fallen—and she'd realized the reason wasn't because he wanted to hop down her bunny trail—she'd wiggled out from under him and taken off his shoes. She'd covered him with a blanket, which he had knocked to the floor, and now he lay there in rabbit form, snuggled up like a little ball of cottony fluff.

She padded barefoot into the living room and sank onto the cushion next to him, her heart sinking along with her body. If she didn't get herself together and fix him, he'd become an animal permanently. No more gazing into his deep, jewel-green eyes. No more pep talks from the Easter Bunny. No more *kissing* the Easter Bunny...

Her sinking stomach fluttered.

She'd told him everything last night, laid out all her flubs and screw-ups before him like a buffet of reasons for him to squash his growing feelings for her and run away.

But he'd stayed.

Not just stayed. He'd acted on his feelings and kissed her. And what a kiss it was. She closed her eyes to play it over again in her mind, her lips curling into a smile of their volition. He'd been gentle yet purposeful, his body and his energy making certain she understood there was nowhere in all the realms he would rather be.

For a moment, she'd felt the same way.

She sipped her coffee and gazed at the sleeping bunny, wariness tightening her eyes. The last time she'd caught feelings for someone, she'd caused a catastrophe. She had no right to entertain the idea of having a romantic relationship with Pete.

Then again, Pete's catastrophe had already

happened. Maybe, if she treaded carefully, she could...

"Why don't you take a picture? It'll last longer."

Destiny shot from the couch and covered her mouth. "You can talk. And in bad clichés!"

The rabbit wiggled his nose, making a snickering sound. "I've been talking to you for days."

"Not in your rabbit form." She waved a hand toward him. "Regular shifters can't talk in their animal forms."

He stretched out his front paws, sticking his furry backside into the air like a downward dog pose. Then he shifted his weight forward and yawned. "I'm not a regular shifter, remember?"

Destiny's eyes widened as his rabbit form morphed into the tall, sexy, fully clothed (unfortunately) man. No, not unfortunately. If she were going to see him naked, she'd rather be the one to disrobe him. Slowly. Piece by piece until the anticipation consumed her. Was it getting hot in there? She fought the urge to fan herself.

"Good morning." He flashed a lopsided smile. "Got any more of that delicious-smelling coffee? Is that a hint of hazelnut I detect?"

"It's pecan." She returned the smile, unable to tear her gaze away from his glittering, otherworldly eyes. One look in the mirror should prove to him he was no run-of-the-mill shifter.

"Mind if I grab a cup?"

"Oh. Yes, I'll get it for you." Finally, she snapped out of her trance and scurried to the kitchen to pour him a mug. "I usually have yogurt with fruit and granola for breakfast...when I'm not binge-eating éclair filling. Is that okay with you?"

"Either sounds delicious." His voice came from right behind her, making her jump.

Coffee sloshed onto the counter, and she set the cup down before spinning around to face him. "You move like a ninja."

"Sorry for scaring you." He pulled a few paper towels off the roll and cleaned up the mess. "How did I end up sleeping on the couch? Last night is foggy."

Her stomach did a weird flip-floppy thing before her abdomen clenched. Last night was foggy? Did he seriously not remember her pulling all the skeletons out of her closet and letting him dance with them?

Did he not remember the kiss?

She swallowed the thickness from her throat and refilled his mug. "You passed out like Crimson said you might do. I gave you a blanket." She handed him the mug.

He sniffed the contents, smiling before taking a sip. "It tastes as good as it smells. That reminds me of something." He flicked his gaze to hers before dropping it to her lips. "Did we kiss last night, or did I dream it?"

A maniacal giggle bubbled up from her chest, and she pressed her fingers to her lips. She could tell him no. Let him believe he dreamed the whole thing. That would be the responsible thing to do. Experience told her mixing business with pleasure worked out as well as baking with salt instead of sugar.

But that would be a lie. Unlike the seraphs in middle management and above, earthbound angels were quite capable of fibbing. Sometimes they had to tell little white lies to help guide people to make good decisions.

But lying to Pete, whether it would help their situation or not, felt wrong. Something deep inside her soul wouldn't allow her to utter a single falsehood to this man.

"I hope it wasn't a dream." He arched a brow, holding her gaze.

"It was real." She cleared her throat and turned to the fridge, busying herself with making breakfast. "I have to go down and work on a few cakes that are being picked up today. Hopefully a bit of normalness will help me think of a way to restore your memories. Though, if Eostre herself couldn't do it, I'm not sure what help I'll be. At the very least, we need a way for you to cross realms so you can deliver the eggs."

"So we're not going to talk about it, then?" He sank into a chair at the table, and she set a bowl in front of him.

"Talk about what?" She sat across from him, stirring her spoon through the yogurt. The kiss had happened. He just said he hoped he didn't dream it, so why was she making things so awkward? *Get yourself together, girl. It's obvious he likes you.*

Her cheeks heated at the thought, and she fought her smile. He did like her. *Very* obviously.

"Destiny." He reached across the table, resting his hand on hers. "Did I go too far? I didn't mean to make you uncomfortable."

"Too far?" She set down her spoon and finally gathered her courage. Flashing a playful grin, she laced her fingers with his and looked into his eyes. "You didn't go too far. I was ready for you to fall down my rabbit hole."

His brows shot toward his hairline, and she ate a spoonful of yogurt, holding his gaze as the butterflies in her stomach choreographed a lively ballet. Yep, she just said that. Out loud. To the Easter Bunny. *Holy fuzz balls.*

He grinned and tugged from her grasp. "It's a shame I passed out. I'd have hopped right to it."

"'Here *Comes* Peter Cottontail' would've had a whole new meaning." She bit her bottom lip as he cringed.

"Too corny. Forget I said that." She shoveled a mound of granola into her mouth to stop herself from talking.

"No, I like a little corn as much as the next guy, but..." His brow furrowed as he stared into his bowl. "I don't like that name. I hate it, actually, but I don't know why." He lifted his gaze to hers, and the knot in her gut untied itself.

"A memory! That's good!" She grabbed her phone from the charger. "Maybe if I play the song for you, it'll knock something loose."

"Don't—"

Too late. She found the song on YouTube half a second before his protest, and it auto-played. No commercial first, since she paid extra for the app to be ad-free. Pete sighed and closed his eyes, his mouth tightening in annoyance as the tune continued.

She swiped the app away before the song could finish. "Anything?"

"Just that I really, *really* hate it. The nickname and especially the song." He spooned another bite into his mouth.

"Interesting." She drummed her fingers on the table. "I wonder what else might stir up something from your past."

She glanced at the wall clock. "Heavens to Beelzebub. I need to get to work."

Yes, there were things far more important for her to deal with than cake, but what else could she do? If neither a witch nor a goddess could make Pete remember how to be the Easter Bunny, her only choice was to try something mundane. Maybe if they just chatted as she fell into the rhythm of her work... She took two massive bites of her breakfast and carried her bowl to the sink.

He followed and placed his bowl next to hers, gripping her hand as she reached for the faucet. "I'll take care of this. You've got cakes to bake."

"I..." She started to protest that he was a guest in her home and shouldn't be doing housework, but she was short on time. "Are you sure?"

"Yep, and who knows? Maybe I'll remember I hate washing dishes too." He winked, and her butterflies danced again.

"Thank you." She laid a dishtowel next to the sink.

"Mind if I hop in your shower before I come down to help you?" He turned on the faucet and rinsed a bowl.

"Of course. Your clothes are still in the dryer. You might set it to the freshen-up cycle if they're too wrinkled." She hesitated at the top of the stairs, turning toward him.

He shut off the faucet and dried his hands on the dishtowel. "I'll be down in just a minute. Everything's going to be okay."

She really, *really* wanted to believe him.

PETE SHOWERED and changed out of his borrowed clothes, folding them neatly and laying them on the bathroom counter before heading downstairs to help the beautiful, sweet, incredibly stressed-out angel who had taken him in.

The staircase ended in the kitchen, and he found Destiny in front of an industrial-sized stand mixer filled with green icing. She angled the mixing paddle up and used a silicon spoon to scrape the frosting off it before twisting the bowl and unlocking it from its base.

"That's a lot of frosting," he said, peering over her shoulder and making her jump.

"Oh, heavens." She set the bowl on the counter next to a series of round cakes. "I need to put a bell on you. No one should move that quietly, the fae included."

"I'll remember to announce my presence next time." He laughed and backed away, giving her room to work while he contemplated her words.

Fae. Destiny wouldn't lie to him. He felt that from the tips of his ears to the fluff on his toes. If she said he was the Easter Bunny, then he was the Easter Bunny. He no longer doubted it, but there was one glaring problem. He still didn't *feel* like a fae. Not that he knew what being a fae felt like, but he needed to figure it out soon.

"Did you know me before this happened?" he asked.

Destiny scooped a blob of icing and spread it onto the biggest section of cake. "Sadly, no."

"Why do you say sadly?"

Her hands moved with otherworldly dexterity

as she covered the sides of the cake, smoothing the frosting until not a single swipe mark remained. She didn't look at him, instead moving on to a smaller section as she spoke. "If it isn't obvious, I kinda like you."

"I kinda like you too. More than kinda."

"I like you a lot." She met his gaze, and a pink blush spread across her cheeks, making his stomach flutter and his rabbit thump.

"What if this isn't me, though? What if, after I get my memories back, I'm not like this at all? What if I'm an asshole?"

Her laugh reminded him of music, soft and cheerful. "I doubt the goddess of spring would have granted you this status if you were an asshole. She seems like a kind, pleasant woman."

That was true. Eostre did seem kind when she visited them last night, but Pete also got the feeling she was hiding something, that the story was much more complex than she'd let on.

"I think this you is the you at your core," Destiny continued. "Everything's been stripped away. No past experiences or traumas are shaping your view of the world right now, so this is the most authentic version of yourself you can be. That won't change."

"I hope not."

"You are who you are." The conviction and sincerity in her eyes made his chest tighten. "And you're…"

"I'm the Easter Bunny," he said, which, sounded so weird he couldn't help but laugh. It also felt… real.

She smiled. "Yes, you are."

A cloud tried to lift in his mind. For a brief… excruciatingly brief…moment, something cleared. A memory or idea or *something* tried to break through. He squeezed his eyes shut, focusing and then blinking rapidly when his pinched-face expression did nothing to help him grab onto it.

"Are you okay?" Destiny asked.

The memory was there, so close…until it wasn't. He shrugged, sighing as his shoulders dropped. "It felt like I was going to remember something for a second there."

"Words have power, so I'm not surprised. Something as simple as saying things aloud can actually bring them to fruition."

"Angel 101?" he teased.

"Exactly." She picked up a section of frosted cake and positioned it on top of the biggest circle.

Words have power… Could it really be that easy? Hell, it was worth a shot. "I'm the Easter Bunny," he said again, willing the light of memory to peek through the fog. "I'm the Easter Bunny."

Destiny continued assembling the cake. "Damn right, you are. You're the Easter Bunny."

"The Easter Bunny is me."

Her laugh was contagious. "He sure is."

"Hi, I'm Pete Hasen, and I'm the Easter Bunny." He held out his hand, and she played along, shaking it.

"Are you sure?" She arched a brow. "I'd like to see some ID."

"No problem, ma'am." He reached into his back pocket and pulled out his wallet.

Destiny's eyes widened as he tugged a faery realm identification card from an inside slot. "Pete!" Her mouth dropped open, and she snatched the card. "Where did this come from?"

"From my..." He frowned at the wallet in his hand. "I don't know. I just reached for it, and it was there."

"You have magic pockets! This is good. You're remembering how to use your powers." She handed the ID to him, and he examined it.

The card listed his name, height, eye color, and an address on Lucky Foot Lane. His photo occupied the top left corner, but seeing his own eyes staring back at him wasn't the strangest thing. "Is that supposed to be my birthday? I think there's a digit missing."

Destiny stood next to him, her shoulder resting against his arm as she peered at the card. "March 1, 316. I supposed that's right."

"That would make me over seventeen hundred years old."

"Mm-hmm." She returned to her cake without batting an eye.

"You don't find that hard to believe?"

"From one immortal being to another, no. Not at all." She filled a bag with white frosting and attached a metal tip to one end. "My half-millennium mark is coming up soon."

He returned the card to his wallet and shoved it into his back pocket, where it completely disappeared. Just like that. "Look at this." He patted his butt and turned around, gesturing for her to do the same. "Feel it."

"That's okay. I don't need to feel your butt." Her cheeks pinkened again as she reached toward his backside, fisting her hand and jerking it away before she cleared her throat. "I can see."

He slipped his hand into it and moved it around. "It's gone."

"Until you need it again. You have some type of glamour magic, which isn't surprising." She filled another icing bag, and a timer pinged across the room.

"No, it's really gone." He tried to grab it from the nothingness in his pocket, but his fingers only brushed the fabric of his pants. "If it were simple glamour, it would still be there."

"Then it's not simple." Destiny strode to the oven and opened the door, a cloud of black smoke billowing out as she bent down. "Oh, dear. Oh, no!"

TWELVE

"I set the oven too hot." Because of course she did. Gabriela probably thought she was doing the world a favor by binding Destiny's powers. But Destiny didn't need magic to be a world-class screw-up. No, she did just fine at that job whether she could use her magic or not.

She fanned the smoke with an oven mitt and reached inside to grab the pan with her bare hand. "Ow! Dammit!"

Searing pain sliced through her palm, and she yanked her hand back, dropping the mitt and gripping her wrist. *Use your brain, Destiny. Angels aren't heatproof.*

"Are you okay?" Pete rushed toward her and

examined the burn. "Oof. That looks angry. I hope angels heal quickly."

"We do." She waved off his concern and reached for the mitt.

He beat her to it and safely pulled the burned bread pudding from the oven. "It helps if you actually wear them." He winked and set the offending pan on a hotplate before dropping the mitt on the counter. "All better?"

She eyed the wounds on her palm and fingers. Normally, a burn like this would be healed within sixty seconds. But not this time. No, this time her skin screamed with pain, and blisters bubbled on her fingertips. "When Gabriela bound my powers, she apparently bound everything. My healing ability included."

Pete frowned at her hand and gently cradled it in his. "Do you have a first aid kit?"

"No. I've never needed one."

"You'll need a bandage and some ointment." He shoved his hands into his front pockets and pulled out both, his feat of magic not even registering as he smoothed the medicine onto her hand and wrapped it in gauze.

The pain cooled immediately, but the fact his medicine obviously had magical properties wasn't what had her in awe. "Pete, you pulled that from thin air."

He chuckled and returned the items to his pockets, where they disappeared instantly. "More like from a cotton/poly blend."

"And you have no idea how you did it? Can you do it again?"

He reached in and shrugged. "I suppose I just needed it, so it was there. It's gone now." He used the oven mitt to dump the burnt bread pudding into the trash. "Was that for an order?"

"Shoot. Yes, it was. I'll have to make more." She scurried to the pantry to gather the ingredients. "Between this and the cakes, it's going to take me all day. If you want to go for a walk or watch television, that's fine. I'm afraid I won't be much company until the orders are filled." She set a loaf of French bread on a cutting board and took a serrated knife from the block.

"Let me help you. What can I do first?"

"I've got it." She sawed into the slightly stale bread, cutting it into small pieces. "I should've paid more attention to the oven temperature. I screwed it up, so I'll fix it."

"Destiny." He stepped behind her, giving her shoulders a squeeze. "It's okay to make mistakes, and it's okay to let people help you. Especially when you're injured."

Warmth radiated from his body, and she closed her eyes for a long blink, giving herself three full seconds to enjoy the sensation before stepping out of his embrace. "Spending all day cooped up in my bakery won't help you get your memories back."

"If I help you, it won't take all day." He carried the now-empty pan to the sink and started to wash it.

He wasn't wrong. Together, they could work at twice the speed, and maybe, just maybe...

"Put that down. I have an idea." She strode toward the four-tiered cake she'd begun frosting before the bread pudding disaster and filled a bag with gold icing. "You can help by decorating this cake."

"I'm afraid I don't know the first thing about cake decorating." He dried his hands and strode toward her.

"It's easy. Here are all the icing tips." She gestured to the box of little silver tips and set a sheet of laminated paper next to it. "This illustrates how the icing will look coming out of each one, and this is what you're making."

She tapped a tablet screen and pulled up the

image the customer had submitted. "It's for a St. Patrick's Day party happening tonight. Green, white, and gold. Argyle pattern on the bottom layer, draw some shamrocks on the others, and top it with a little pot of gold. It's art. You're an artist. You can even make a little fondant rainbow if you want to jazz it up."

He stilled, staring at the partially frosted cake. "I don't remember being an artist."

"It'll come back to you." She pressed a bag of green frosting into his hand. "Like riding a bike." Or so she hoped. If she could get him designing again, shifting his thoughts away from trying to remember his past and focusing them on creating art, maybe something might come to him.

His brow furrowed, his gaze cutting between the cake, the icing bag, and the example image, but still, he didn't move.

"Like this." She took his hand and guided it to the counter, squeezing the bag and creating a star-shaped blob of green. "And if you move your hand while you squeeze..." She guided him to the right, lifting and pushing back to make a series of shell shapes. "That's what the bottom border should look like."

He blinked, a strange expression overtaking his

features that Destiny hoped to heaven was the look of a memory jogging loose. "Yeah. Okay, I can do this."

She backed away slowly so she didn't spook whatever his brain was attempting to conjure and grabbed another loaf of bread to start the pudding recipe again. Her hand tingled, and she peeked beneath the bandage. Whatever ointment he'd pulled from his magical pocket was a miracle unto itself. Her burns had completely healed. *So cool.*

She tossed the gauze into the trash and chuckled as she imagined all the women of the world having pockets like Pete's, being able to access whatever they needed, whenever they needed it. Now that was a miracle-worthy endeavor. Hell, most women would be thrilled for their pants to be blessed with pockets they could fit a cellphone in. Or at least a full set of keys.

Fifteen minutes passed as she worked on the recipe, and she put a new pan of pudding into the oven, double-checking the temperature so she didn't burn it again. She set the timer and checked the computer for the next order before glancing at Pete, who put the final swirl on the top layer of cake.

"Done," he said, and he set the icing bag on the counter. "What's next?"

Destiny peered at his creation and padded toward him. The cake looked magnificent, the lines clean, the shamrocks virtually perfect. "You did this whole thing in fifteen minutes."

She parked her hands on her hips and admired his work. It would have taken her at least an hour to pull off something this elaborate, and that was when she had access to her magic. He'd even added flakes of edible glitter to highlight the gold coins. She hadn't given him any glitter. Did he pull that out of the cotton/poly blend too?

"It took me a minute to get used to the pressure. The next one should be faster." He wiped the back of his hand across his cheek, smudging himself with gold icing.

"Faster?" She laughed and wiped his face with a hand towel. "At this rate, we'll be done before lunchtime."

"I'm okay with that." His gaze dropped to her mouth before flicking back to her eyes. "Then we can finish what we started before I blacked out."

Her stomach looped, but she managed to cut off the maniacal giggle before it escaped her throat. That idea sounded way better than lunch. Heat crept up her neck as she held his gaze, and her pulse quickened. Was it bad that she considered saying to hell with the cakes and taking him upstairs right then and there?

Yes, Destiny. You've got customers counting on you. Realms, even. Still, it was a fun idea to entertain.

"We'll see about that." She playfully slapped the towel against his stomach and headed for the walk-in fridge to cool herself off. Holy hellhounds in a handbasket. If their chemistry got any hotter, she'd short-circuit the entire city.

She took a deep breath, letting the chilled air center her. Next up was a full sheet cake with psychedelic swirls in a pallet straight from the seventies. She'd baked the cakes in advance, using her angel magic to preserve them, so frosting was the only step left.

"Grab the tablet and pull up order one sixty-two." She carried the cake to the table before retrieving tubs of brown, yellow, and orange icing. "This one is for an adult birthday, and when you're done, you can start on one sixty-three if you like."

He arched a brow at the screen. "These are the colors they want?"

"Yep. Exactly those, but you have freedom in the design. Swirl and twirl however you want."

He grinned. "On it."

Destiny mixed a white chocolate sauce, letting it

cool before putting it into a plastic container. The oven timer dinged, and she pulled out the bread pudding, perfectly baked this time, and set it on a rack before turning to Pete.

"How's it go...ing?" Her brows shot toward her hairline. In the half-hour it had taken her to finish the pudding, he'd frosted three cakes and hand-decorated six dozen sugar cookies for an order that had apparently come in eight minutes ago. "How in heaven do you move so fast?"

"I have to. How else could I get billions of eggs ready for delivery in two weeks' time?" His brown slammed down over his eyes. "I have help. We're all fast. They... I..." He set down the icing bag and scratched his head. "I think I have a team. I...I don't know."

"Pete!" She rushed toward him, taking his face in her hands before clutching his shoulders. "Focus. The eggs. You paint billions?"

His eyes tightened, his forehead creasing as he concentrated. He squeezed his lids shut, his lips pursing until he finally sighed. "I can't remember. I lost it."

"It's okay." She wrapped her arms around him, pulling him into a hug. "Your memories are there.

We just have to knock them loose, and I promise you it will be my only focus until it's done."

"It can't be your only focus." He tried to break the hug, but she held him tighter.

"It can and it will be. I'm going to make this right."

"Destiny." He gripped her shoulders, gently pushing her away. "My life isn't the only one at stake. What about your miracle? You need to focus on that too."

"Well, I can't miracle your memories back. I tried." She shrugged out of his embrace. "I honestly can't think of anything else that might get approved, so I'm just going to do my best to help you. At the very least, if I have to grow old and die, I can do it knowing I did everything in my power to help you save your realm."

"No, I don't like that. There has to be a way." He tapped a finger to his lips. "The prophecy said I would leave my land to devise a plan. If I came here to ask Gaston for help, I have a feeling my plan was to take him to Eostre's realm to investigate. Can that be your miracle? Sending a fae and a vampire across realms?"

She pouted her lips, contemplating Gabriela's

likely response to a request like that. Maybe if she worded it just right, she could... Her shoulders slumped. Who was she kidding? "You're a fae. The ability to cross realms is ingrained in your soul. Gabriela wouldn't find that miracle-worthy. I doubt the request would make it past her assistant's desk."

"Are you sure? Because Eostre is a goddess, and even she couldn't drag me across. If a goddess couldn't make it happen, it sounds like it would take a miracle to get me there."

Destiny shook her head. "Eostre said she couldn't take you because you have to *remember* how to cross the realms yourself. Your lack of memory is my fault. I can't request a miracle to remedy my own mistake."

A conspiratorial grin lifted his lips. "Eostre said *she* can't get me across unless I remember."

"So?"

"So, that means it really would take a miracle. I might not remember how to be the Easter Bunny, but you can bet your shiny gold halo I know how to improvise. Get me to Eostre's realm, and I'll figure the rest out from there. It might be with goose eggs this year, but we will make Easter happen."

She sucked in a sharp breath. "You're right. I'm

not asking to make you remember how to cross realms. I'm asking to send you there myself."

"Exactly." He set her laptop in front of her. "We can do this together. You and me."

"Together. Eostre said that was the only way we could fix things." She logged in to the miracle network and cracked her knuckles.

She typed furiously, backspacing and rewording to make certain no mention or vague reference to Pete's missing memories remained in her request. She didn't ask to save Easter either. This request was all new and precisely specific. Send Pete to the fae realm. That was all. The fewer details she gave, the more likely it would pass through.

When she finished, she read it four more times. "I told them I know the ability is ingrained in your soul, but you can't access it. Souls are a big deal to angels, so that should get their attention." Plus, angels hated the fae. Shipping one back to his own realm should sound appealing enough.

Her pulse racing, she hovered her finger above the enter key and flicked her gaze to Pete. "Together?"

He smiled and laid his hand over hers. "Together."

They pressed the button, sending the miracle

request into the ether. Her breath came out in a rush, and she closed the laptop before turning around.

Pete stood facing her, his otherworldly eyes glittering. "Feels good to find a solution, doesn't it?"

"I don't know about good. I'm still a nervous wreck. The waiting is the hardest part." Because they could be stuck waiting until their time ran out.

He stepped toward her, brushing the back of his fingers across her cheek. "Then let me take your mind off it."

THIRTEEN

Pete couldn't pinpoint exactly what came over him in that moment. The shred of memory he'd recovered had been so fleeting, he'd already lost it. Decorating the cakes had been a blast. Using colors and shapes to create intricate, edible designs felt as much a part of him as the whiskers on his rabbit's nose, and that was cool and all. But it was more than that.

He'd decorated those cakes for Destiny. They had fulfilled her orders together. They'd come up with a plan to both save her wings and the fae realm together, and that was exactly what it was.

Together was where they belonged, whether it was here, creating edible art, in the fae realm stopping a vampire, or upstairs in the bedroom, where he planned to spend as much time with her as possible, now and in whatever amount of future they had left.

He cupped her cheek in his hand, and she nuzzled against it, closing her eyes. "Pete."

"That's my name…or so I'm told." He gently straightened her head, drawing her gaze to his.

"You still don't remember anything?" she asked.

"It doesn't matter." He glided his other hand across her shoulder. "All your orders for today have been filled. We've got a few hours before anyone arrives to pick them up, so let's make the most of it."

She swallowed hard, confliction tightening her eyes. "Last time I got involved with a charge…"

"This isn't last time, and I'm not your charge." He leaned in, taking her mouth with his.

She tasted as sweet as he remembered, like a little piece of heaven made just for him, and as she wrapped her arms around him, her body seemed to mold to his, her soft curves filling in his sharp angles, making him whole.

A soft moan vibrated across her lips, and she clutched his shirt, tugging the hem upward before sliding her hands beneath it. The feel of her soft skin on his stomach made his muscles contract, tightening from his chest to his groin.

She giggled. "You don't have to flex for me."

He laughed. "You seem to have that effect on me."

She glided her hands up to his chest and down again before running a single finger over the waistband of his pants. Every muscle in his body clenched so tightly, he could've cracked a pecan between his butt cheeks.

"Are you okay?" She let his shirt fall over his abs, and he could breathe again.

"It's taking every ounce of my strength to not swipe my arm across this table, knock all the cakes to the ground, and take you right here."

"Hmm." She grinned. "It would be a shame to destroy all your hard work. Maybe you should take me upstairs."

She didn't have to ask him twice. With one arm across her back, he scooped her into a cradle carry and headed for the stairs, taking them two at a time. When he reached the top, he set her down and grasped her hand between both of his.

"Are you sure you want to do this?" He kissed the inside of her wrist, and her breath hitched before she smiled slyly.

"We have to pass the time somehow." She winked. "Hop to it, Mr. Rabbit."

Heat unfurled in his belly, settling into his dick and hardening it like a rod. He would happily spend forever doing this with her. Doing everything with her.

A sinking sensation formed in his stomach. All joking aside, he needed to be sure she understood that what he had planned was entirely against the rules. "Angels and fae aren't supposed to have relations. Everyone knows that, even bunnies with amnesia."

"I know, but..." Her brow pinched, the look of rejection in her eyes nearly crumbling him. "Are you saying you don't want to?"

"No, not at all." He pulled her to his chest. "I think we've established how I feel about rules. I don't give a fluff about ridiculous laws made eons ago, but you do. You could get into trouble."

"Oh, angels are forbidden from fornicating with the fae." She rested her hands on his shoulders and leaned back to gaze into his eyes. "But my powers are bound. I'm essentially human right now, and anyway..."

"Fluff the rules?" He grinned.

She nodded. "Fluff the rules."

Clutching his hand, she led him down a short hallway and into her bedroom. A buttercream yellow duvet covered her bed, and matching sheer curtains hung over the bay window, warming the sunlight's hue as it filtered through. Pastel pillows adorned the window seat, and a small shelf filled with paperbacks stood adjacent to it.

She's mine, his rabbit said in his mind. *I'm working on it, buddy.* He cleared his throat. "That's a nice reading nook."

"I like the lighting." She rested her hands against his chest. "I also like you."

"Mmm…" He tucked a lock of coppery hair behind her ear. "That makes me a happy bunny."

"How happy?" She ran her hands downward, but he caught them before they could reach their destination.

"I'm about to show you." He gripped the back of his shirt and tugged it over his head.

She parted her lips as her gaze wandered down his form and up again. When her eyes met his, he could have sworn he saw forever inside them.

He closed the distance between them and moved her long hair aside to reach for her zipper. He slid it down and slipped his fingers beneath the shoulder straps, pulling them forward until her dress fell to the floor.

She wore a pink satin bra and matching panties

beneath, and his heart thumped in his chest, pumping even more blood into his groin.

Mate, his rabbit reminded him. *Yes. Yes, indeed.*

He took her in his arms and crushed his mouth to hers. With a flick of his fingers, he unhooked her bra, and she threw it aside before leaning into him. Her skin was warm, silky soft against his, the sensation blinding him with desire. He needed Destiny like he'd never needed anything in his life.

She kicked off her shoes as he kissed her, and he did the same, fumbling with the button on his pants at the same time. Destiny laughed against his lips, never breaking the kiss as she popped it open and slid his zipper down.

Before he could work his pants over his hips, she reached into them, gripping his dick through his underwear. It throbbed in response, aching to be set free. Hooking his thumbs into the waistbands, he shoved the rest of his clothes to the floor and kicked them aside.

Destiny took a step backward, her gaze locking on his groin. "Very happy, I see."

"You have no idea." He moved toward her and grabbed her ass before sliding his hands to the backs of her thighs and lifting her from the floor. She fell backward onto the bed, her squeal turning into a delightful giggle and she shimmied to the center of the mattress.

A ray of sunlight fell across her body, giving her an ethereal glow, despite her lack of magic. Her hair glittered, and her blue eyes shown in a way that only his fated mate's could. He inhaled deeply, her arousal tinting the sweet vanilla-lavender scent of her skin and making his mouth water.

He joined her on the bed, slipping her panties off, giving himself access to every magnificent part of her. He lay atop her, nuzzling into her neck, basking in her glory. "You are the most beautiful creature I have ever seen."

He kissed her cheek, her lips, the hollow dip at the base of her neck. Trailing his lips downward, he kissed between her breasts before moving to a nipple. As he sucked the delicate pearl into his mouth, she inhaled a quick breath.

"Is it true what they say about rabbits?" She tangled her fingers in his hair.

"That we can multiply like nobody's business? Yeah, but lucky for us, angels and fae can't reproduce." He flicked out his tongue, bathing her other nipple before giving it a light nip with his teeth.

She let out a slow, satisfied hiss. "I meant the battery commercial."

He chuckled and rose onto his hands. "That we keep going..."

"And going, and going..." Her voice was breathy, the desire in her eyes almost more than he could take. Almost...

"You'll just have to wait and see." He kissed his way down her stomach, spreading her legs and settling his shoulders between them. "First I want to know if you taste as sweet as you look."

He swiped his tongue up her center, pausing on her clit and circling it twice.

She gasped and gripped the sheets. "And?"

"Undetermined. I think I need another taste." He bathed her sensitive nub in wet heat, making her moan. "Mmm... I'll definitely need more than a few bites." He licked her again, sucking her clit between his lips and working circles with his tongue.

"Ohhh..." she said, though it was more breath than word. "Oh, Pete."

He moaned against her, slipping two fingers inside her, and she writhed in pleasure beneath him, every sound she made, every breath she breathed turning him on in a way he was absolutely certain he had never experienced before.

She belonged to him.

And it was his duty to please her.

She cried out his name again, arching her back as her climax overtook her. He continued licking and sucking as she rode the wave until she pitched forward and gripped his shoulders.

"I need you inside me. Please."

"I will give you everything you need." He covered her body with his and plunged inside her with one swift thrust.

She gasped and wrapped her legs around him, taking him in deeper, squeezing him. He pulled out slowly and slid back in, reveling in the sounds she made as he moved. The entire world and all the realms ceased to exist in that moment. He and she were all that remained, she all he would ever need.

He continued thrusting, listening, watching, angling his hips according to her responses until she climaxed again. He started to rise onto his hands, but she clutched his shoulders, holding him close as she orgasmed.

"Come for me, Pete," she whispered against his ear, and that was all it took.

He slammed into her, grinding against her center as his own release overtook him. Stars danced in his vision, and, when he squeezed his eyes shut, they grew brighter. He panted, her breaths matching his until they slowed to a normal rhythm.

As she loosened her grip on his shoulders, he held her tighter, unable to let her go. She relaxed beneath him, gliding her fingers over his sweat-slickened back and turning her head to kiss his cheek.

"Mine," he said aloud this time. He didn't mean to, but his rabbit was so adamant, the word just slipped out.

"What?" Destiny wiggled beneath him, so he rolled off and pushed to sitting.

"That, ah..." He rubbed the back of his neck. "I'm sorry. That was my rabbit talking. He really, *really* likes you. He wants you to be mine...my mate."

His stomach looped, and he clamped his mouth shut. What the ever-loving fluff was he thinking? So much for easing her into the idea.

"And you?" She sat up, touching his shoulder as she scooted closer. "How does the man feel?"

He took a deep breath, chewing the inside of his cheek. He was all in. There was no denying it, so he might as well tell her. "Everything about you feels right. I want you to be mine too." He held his breath as he awaited her response.

She nipped her bottom lip between her teeth

and searched his eyes, swallowing hard before she spoke. "As crazy as it sounds, I'm good with that. Logic tells me it simply can't be, but I know in my heart...in my soul...that we are meant to be together forever, whether our forever lasts two more weeks or an eternity."

He cupped her cheek, gliding his thumb over her soft lips. "You have no idea how happy you just made me."

She glanced at his dick, still standing at attention. "Maybe you should show me."

"Maybe I should." He laid her back on the bed.

She grinned. "So you can keep going."

"And going." He brushed his lips over hers and was about to show her just how long he could go when a thunderous crash sounded from below.

Destiny gasped and pressed a hand to her chest. "That came from my bakery."

FOURTEEN

Destiny scrambled to put on her clothes, not bothering with shoes before she and Pete darted downstairs to the sounds of metal clanking and crashing and glass shattering. She reached for the door separating the bakery from her home, but Pete caught her wrist.

"Wait," he whispered. "They might be armed."

"So? I can't let them destroy my bakery." She tried to tug from his grasp, but he turned her hand over and ran his fingertips over her palm.

"I don't know if my magical salve can fix a bullet wound. We have to be smart." He let her go, and she clutched her hand, brushing her thumb over the spot that used to be blistered and burned.

He scooted past her and cracked open the door,

flattening himself against the wall as he peered into the kitchen. His brow scrunched, and he leaned forward, pushing the door slightly more ajar.

"What do you see?" She clutched his arm, using all her will to keep herself from busting through and throwing herself in harm's way. If a hot pan could burn her as badly as it had, she didn't want to think about getting her butt kicked. "It's a demon, isn't it? I bet it's Richard. He's the most gluttonous famine demon I've ever met."

"I'm not sure." Pressing a finger to his lips, he pushed the door all the way open, and of course it creaked on its hinges, alerting the intruder just like in the movies.

The culprit let out a startled squawk-squeal, and Destiny heard the distinct sound of feathers rustling before a metal shelving unit, filled with dozens of empty cake pans and baking sheets, crashed to the floor.

Pete stepped into the kitchen, holding an arm out as if to shield her as she followed. When she saw the state of disarray her beloved bakery lay in, you could bet your sweet blood pudding Destiny wasn't the one who needed protection. She'd never been so livid in her entire existence.

Not a single tool, pan, or pot remained on the

shelves. Everything she owned lay busted on the floor. The intruder had turned circular cake pans into smushed ovals, shattered her tablet screen, and broken her laptop into three pieces.

They'd swiped the beautiful cakes Pete had decorated off the table, and now all his work lay in colorful blobs on the floor, and... *Oh, lovely.* The sheet cake had a butt print right in the center of the psychedelic swirls.

But that wasn't even the worst of it.

Her gaze landed on the wide-open door to the walk-in fridge, and her breath caught. Her throat thickened as she stepped over the butt cake, a sense of dread settling in her stomach like a two-pound fruitcake.

"Oh, please no." She took two cautious steps forward and froze. All two-weeks' worth of angel food cakes—the very things that kept the demons of New Orleans at bay—lay crumbled on the floor. Whoever broke in had mashed the light, airy cakes into nearly nothing and poured vegetable oil and vinegar over the mess, making certain they were inedible.

"I didn't see anyone in the shop, and the front door is still locked. They must have run out the back." Pete rested a hand on the small of her back. "Oh, damn. Are those..."

"All that was left of the angel food cakes? Yeah. And with my magic bound, I can't make more. I don't..." She turned in a circle, taking in the messy scene, and a sob rolled up from her chest. Pressure built in her eyes, and she pressed her hands to her cheeks as the tears rolled down.

"I'm done. It's over." She sniffled and sobbed again, half from distress and the other half from the sheer anger burning in her veins.

"Hey, don't say that. We'll figure this out." He rubbed her back, and she shrugged away.

"Please, I can't handle one of your peppy pep talks right now. As soon as Gabriela finds out, she'll send another angel to swoop in and take over, and I'll be kicked to the curb. And not even a pretty Garden District curb. No, I'll land in a puddle of pee on Bourbon Street outside a seedy strip club at three A.M."

He had the nerve to laugh. "Well, that sounds awful."

"It isn't funny, Pete."

"No, you're right." He raised his hands. "What happened isn't funny, but we can fix it. Your boss doesn't need to know."

"I have to take care of the demons. It's my job to keep the balance." She gasped. "'Balance dies. Destiny is awry.' What if the prophecy really is about me...about the balance here in New Orleans, and not in the fae realm?"

He frowned. "I don't think fae gods would concern themselves with angel problems."

"No, I guess not. This..." She exhaled and gestured to the mess. "This is personal. Someone sabotaged me. Why would they...?" The anger sparking in her chest turned into a raging fire as the realization sank in.

She clenched her teeth, grinding them until her jaw ached. "Gabriela did this."

Pete's frown deepened, and he righted a toppled shelving unit, scooting it back into place. "Do angels commit sabotage? That sounds like it would be very against the rules."

"It is, but Gabriela has been out to get me since my first screwup. The only reason I haven't been wasting away in the repository for centuries is that Michelle wouldn't let her send me there."

He picked up a pan and tried to bend it back into shape. "I don't know. A demon seems the more likely culprit."

"I heard feathers. Wings rustling. Demon wings

are leathery, not feathery." She tapped her tablet screen, waking it up so she could send her boss a scathing email. She'd CC Michelle, too, just to be certain the higher ups knew. "She's making sure she never has to deal with me again. Dammit." She couldn't see anything on the shattered screen. "I need to get my phone."

"Hold on. Let's think about this." He picked up a baking sheet and set it on the shelf. "Wouldn't it be easier for Gabriela just to reject your miracle requests? Why would she go to all this trouble?"

"Because she's extra like that." Destiny crossed her arms, digging in her heels, but Pete did have a point. Gabriela rarely left her office.

"It wasn't an angel," a tiny, disembodied voice said.

Destiny snapped her gaze in the direction of the sound. Her industrial stand mixer, too bulky and heavy for the culprit to knock over, stood in the corner. She marched toward it, and two teensy hands gripped the edge of the icing vat before a blob of green frosting with big black eyes peered over it.

"Gremlin!" She lunged toward the mixer, flipping the switch to turn it on high and backpedaling as quickly as her feet would take her, which was, apparently, too quick.

Her heel landed on a rolling pin, and her leg slipped out from under her. She stumbled, her attempt to catch herself on the edge of the table only making matters worse.

Her hand landed in a smear of frosting and slipped across the surface. Her head smacked the edge, and she bounced off, careening backward and landing in a mound of smashed cake.

The nasty little gremlin grunted and squealed as he went round and round in the mixer. Frosting flew from the bowl, inertia forcing the creature higher and higher up the edges until he sailed across the room and hit the wall with a *thunk*. He made an *errrrr* sound as he slid to the floor, and Destiny sat up, clutching her aching head.

"Are you okay?" Pete kneeled beside her, taking her head in his hands and examining her. He brushed her hair from her forehead and grimaced. "You've got a lump the size of a chocolate cream egg."

"I'll be fine." Humiliation would do her in long before a bump on her head ever could. She hauled herself to her feet, being careful not to slip in the mess. "We have to catch the gremlin before he destroys the whole building."

Pete tilted his head and narrowed his eyes at the

creature in question. "Are you sure that's a gremlin? It looks like a raccoon to me."

She followed his gaze and found, not the leathery green, toad-like creature she expected, but a furry, masked critter who was probably fluffy and cuddly when his fur wasn't matted with frosting.

The raccoon used his tiny paws to wipe his face. He sniffed the green icing on his fingers and gave them a lick, his eyes widening as he nodded and continued to clean himself. He wiped his little snoot, and when his face was as clean as he could get it without a bath, he stood and waddled toward Pete.

"Mr. Hasen, sir. It's so good to see you." He bowed his head before turning to Destiny. "Ma'am."

She stared at the creature and blinked. Raccoons couldn't talk. Not in this realm, anyway. Squinting, she tried to read his aura, but with her magic bound, she couldn't tell the difference between a demon and a dessert tray.

The critter was either enchanted by a witch or he was a fae. After all she'd been through, Destiny would put her money on the latter. She snatched the rolling pin she'd slipped on and held it toward him as threateningly as she could.

"Why did you destroy my bakery?" She moved

to stand next to Pete, trying her damnedest not to slip again.

"I didn't." He picked a blob of frosting from his arm and flicked it to the floor. "Mr. Rabbit, you know I would never do something like this."

"I do?" Pete's face scrunched. "Who are you?"

The raccoon sighed, his posture slumping. "Eostre warned me you might not remember me. I'm Max, the lead *elfen* in your egg studio. You've known me for going on a thousand years."

"A thousand years." He continued staring at Max, no doubt trying to force the memory to surface.

Destiny waited fifteen seconds. When Pete didn't have the *ah-ha* moment he was searching for, she waved the rolling pin. "If you didn't do this, who did?"

"It was Helga." Max eyed Pete warily. "You remember her, right? The poultry thorn in your side?"

He shifted his gaze up and to the right as if someone in the ether might send the memories down to him. "Sorry." He rubbed the back of his neck. "I don't remember anything."

"Who's Helga?" Destiny loosened her grip on the rolling pin. Her ability to read auras and tap into the collective consciousness might be bound more tightly than a baby in a bunting, but she was still an excellent judge of character. Max seemed sincere, and the concerned expression on his fuzzy little face told her he meant no harm.

He combed more frosting from his fur. "May I borrow your sink?"

"Of course." Where were her manners? "Right over here."

Max walked on his hind legs to the sink and stood on his tippy toes, stretching both arms up toward the ledge. When he couldn't reach, he tried one arm and then the other.

"Would you like some help?" Destiny asked. "I can lift you."

He turned toward her. "That would be nice. Thank you."

"My pleasure." She smiled softly and picked him up, placing him in the sink before turning on the water.

"Max," Pete mumbled. "Helga. Didn't Eostre say something about Helga?"

"Oh, yeah. That's why the name sounds famil-iar." Destiny handed Max the spray nozzle. "She said Helga offered to help. That her geese flock would lay the eggs."

Max snorted and squeezed the sprayer, rinsing his face and chest. "Helga isn't helping. She's trying to take over."

"To take over Easter?" Destiny wiped her hands on a dishtowel.

"Yep. Would you mind getting my back?" Max offered the sprayer. "She has all Pete's *elfen* locked in the studio, and she's forcing them to use stencils to paint the eggs."

"Stencils?" Pete's lip curled. "But then they'll all look the same."

"I know, sir. It's a travesty." Max turned around, and Destiny sprayed water on his back, using her fingers to work out the icing clumps.

With Max's fur clean and frosting-free, Destiny grabbed a clean dishtowel and dried him before setting him on the floor. He gave his body a shake, and his damp fur fluffed out, turning him into a little poof ball.

She set the towel on the counter, her face pinching as she tried to make sense of his story. "How does destroying my bakery help Helga take over Easter? And why were you hiding in a vat of frosting?"

"Stencils." Pete scoffed and crossed his arms. "How many different designs?"

"Just one, sir. One stencil for billions of eggs, and she doubled everyone's quotas. She's working them to the bone."

Pete shook his head like he couldn't believe what he'd heard. "How can I help?"

"Hold on." Destiny raised her hands. Stencils were the least of her worries. "I need you to start from the beginning because none of this makes sense."

Max climbed onto a stool, getting closer to their eye level. "A vampire is killing the hens. The rest are too stressed to lay eggs, so Pete came to this realm to get help from his vampire friend. But he ended up with amnesia."

"I know that much. I'm the one who gave it to him." She leaned against the counter and crossed her arms.

"Helga, the golden goose, offered her supposed help," Max continued, "and Eostre agreed to let her supply the eggs. That's all she agreed to, but..."

He looked at Pete, his eyes full of sympathy. "Before Eostre allowed Helga into the studio, she asked me to keep an eye on her. She thought something about her had changed, but she didn't know what. I haven't been able to reach Eostre since. She doesn't answer my calls. She doesn't check in at the studio. I don't know where she is."

"So, Helga has hijacked Easter, and Eostre is MIA." She drummed her fingers against her biceps. "What does my bakery have to do with any of that?"

"Right." Pete wrapped an arm around her waist. "There are too many pieces missing from this puzzle."

"Eostre recognized your bond when she visited this realm," Max said. "She told me about it, and I'm certain she told Frigg too. Helga must have overheard and come here to sabotage you. She's always been jealous of Pete and anyone close to him."

"So, she did all this because she wants to be the Easter Bunny? Because she wants Pete's job?" Jealousy was the ugliest of emotions, but Destiny still couldn't fathom her reasons. "Did you date her?"

His lip curled in revulsion. "Never."

"Are you sure?" she asked. "Your memory isn't what it used to be."

He opened his mouth to defend his answer, but he paused, his brow furrowing before he shook his head. "I'm positive. The thought of it makes my stomach turn."

"He has never and would never," Max said. "And though I don't doubt she's also jealous of you for winning his affections, her intention here was to make him feel the need to protect you."

"Because if you return to your realm, you can reclaim Easter." She rested a hand on Pete's chest. "She's trying to keep you here."

He nodded. "She knows there's no way in all the realms I would leave you alone with the culprit still on the loose. That's one smart goose."

"And take a gander at this," Max said. "I've been following her, which is why I'm here. Helga has been in cahoots with beings from your realm. She's gotten powers she shouldn't have, and I've seen her drink blood."

"Blood," Pete said, and Max nodded his head.

"Helga the fae golden goose was turned into a vampire?" Destiny rubbed her chin, smearing frosting onto her face. "That would explain how a vamp crossed into your realm, but..." She gestured at the mess and then at the window. "It's daylight. How could she be out in the middle of the day?"

Pete offered her a towel. "She's still a fae. Maybe that's the difference. Can she shift to a human form?"

"Not that I've seen," Max said. "But she's unnaturally strong and ornerier than a rabid honey badger. I hid in the mixer bowl because it was the only thing heavy enough to withstand her strength. I didn't realize it was full until I dove in."

"I'm still trying to wrap my mind around this." Destiny wiped her face and hands. "Helga destroyed my bakery, hoping I'd blame it on someone else and feel unsafe in my own home."

"Exactly." Max nodded. "Because the mating bond between fae is unbreakable. Pete will never leave your side."

"That's true," Pete said. "Whether our bond is fae, shifter, or plain old man to woman, nothing is going to happen to you on my watch."

Good gravy. This mess was thickening like someone added way too much cornstarch to...well, to the gravy. Still, her stomach did flutter a bit at Max's mention of an unbreakable mating bond and Pete's adamant confirmation that it was true. She could appreciate silver linings, no matter how big and messy the cloud.

"You have to come home, sir. The *elfen* need you. Eostre too."

Pete shook his head. "Destiny needs me here."

She gazed at the mess Helga had made of her bakery. There was no possible way she could clean it up and redo the orders on her own, but honestly?

The world wouldn't end if a sixty-year-old didn't get her psychedelic birthday cake.

The only truly life-altering malady that had come from this was the angel food cake stash being destroyed. They had a few days at most until the demons started running amuck, and, as much as it pained her, she needed to get ahold of Gabriela so she could send someone else to bake more.

"I need to use the computer out front. I'll be right back." She padded through the kitchen door into the shop area and powered up the desktop on the counter. As the computer whirred to life, a thud sounded from a cabinet beneath the display case.

Her pulse raced, but before she could move, an ear-piercing squawk sounded from below and a white goose with blood-red eyes and a set of dispro-portionally large fangs leaped onto the counter.

Destiny gasped. "Helga."

The goose squawked again and sprung, sinking her fangs into Destiny's neck.

CHAPTER

FIFTEEN

Squawk! Pete snapped his head toward the door, his heart rate kicking into a sprint. Rabbits were prey animals. Under normal circumstances, his instinct would've chosen flight or freeze, but not this time. When Destiny was in danger, fight was the only option.

He took off toward the door, slipping in a blob of cake mush and catching himself on the counter before he lost his footing. Righting himself, he grabbed a bread knife and plowed through the door, ready to skewer Helga and make goose kabobs with her carcass.

No one threatened *his* angel.

He darted past the counter and spun in a circle. Sunlight streamed in through the windows, and the front door stood ajar. Destiny was nowhere in sight.

His sprinting heart clawed its way into his throat as he flung open the bathroom door. Empty. He checked behind the counter and opened the cupboards. Nothing.

"Destiny?" He jogged out the front door, past the picket fence, shielding his eyes against the midday sun. A group of women laughed as they exited the restaurant next door, and a tall man in jeans and a black t-shirt walked a Yorkie across the street.

But no Destiny.

His stomach turned, souring, bitter bile creeping up the back of his throat as he made his way back inside. Max sat on the countertop, frowning at a white napkin clutched in his hands.

"It was Helga," Pete said. "Where did she take her?"

"I don't know, sir." He offered the napkin. "I do hope angels are truly immortal."

Pete took the napkin, his heart dropping as the red smear registered. No, it couldn't be blood. It was strawberry sauce. It had to be. Helga the goose-pire did not bite his angel. No way had she taken her away to drain her.

This was Pete's fault. He'd done a sweep of the entire downstairs, but Helga had obviously found a hiding place he hadn't looked into. *Fluff me.* "Where did you get this?"

"There were a few drops on the floor, so I wiped them up. There's also a bit of spatter on the wall." Max pointed to the array of red spots dripping down the pale blue paint. "It looks like she bit into an artery."

Pete's stomach lurched again, his mind conjuring images from a bad B horror movie. He squeezed his eyes shut, shaking his head to chase away the intruding thoughts.

"I have to find her. She's not immortal. Not right now." He marched to the door and yanked it open.

"Where are you going, sir?" Max climbed down from the counter and followed.

"Next door. Helga isn't the only one who can collude with the creatures here." He strode across the lawn toward Mike and Crimson's place and climbed the back steps. Without thinking about the lock, he flung the kitchen door open and hurried inside. The setup was the same as Destiny's, with a door in the back corner covering a staircase that led to the living area upstairs.

"Whoa. No animals in the kitchen," a man in a black apron said.

Max scurried toward Pete and clutched the leg of his pants, so he bent down and scooped him into his arms. "It's okay. He's a fae. Is Crimson upstairs?"

A woman with red hair secured in a tight bun gave the man a quizzical look. "Did he say fae?"

Mike cleared his throat and strode toward them. "He said 'ESA.' That's his emotional support raccoon." He opened the stairway door and gestured for Pete to enter. When they made it upstairs and out of the staff's earshot, he said, "I've got humans in the kitchen. Careful what you say down there."

"Sorry." He set his new—or apparently old— raccoon friend on the floor. "Destiny's been kidnapped. A vampire goose. I have to save her."

"What's going on?" Crimson padded barefoot to the kitchen, drying her hair with a fluffy towel. "Who's this little guy? He's cute."

"My name is Max. It's a pleasure to meet you, ma'am." He held out his paw.

"Oh, you're a fae." Crimson shook his paw and straightened. "Does that mean Pete got his memories back?"

"No, ma'am. I'm afraid not." Max wrung his paws.

"Bummer," Crimson said. "What's this about Destiny being kidnapped?"

She took a bowl from a cabinet and filled it with water as Pete explained the incident in the bakery and how Max had come to warn him. A crystal pendulum hung from a hook above the window, and she stood on her tippy toes to take it down.

"But it's the middle of a sunny day." Mike frowned, his eyes calculating.

"She's a goddess-touched fae goose with no human form," Pete said. "It seems her lack of humanity made her invincible to UV rays."

"Well, if she's in this realm, I'll find her." Crimson held the pendulum above the water bowl and closed her eyes, whispering a prayer before swinging the chain in wide circles. Frown lines creased her forehead.

Pete's hands curled into tight fists, and Max scrambled onto a stool to see the witch work her magic. Mike rubbed his palm on his pants, extinguishing the pale red glow that had formed on his skin.

Seconds turned into minutes, and Pete reminded himself to breathe. Helga the golden goose. Why did she sound so familiar to him? Surely, they weren't friends in the past. He would never associate with someone who would abuse the *elfen* like Max had described. And what had the raccoon called her? The poultry thorn in his side?

"She's hidden well," Crimson finally said. "I've asked my guides for help finding them both, but angels and fae are elusive. Since they aren't native to this realm, they aren't grounded here."

All the blood from his upper body plummeted to his feet, making his head spin. If the high priestess of the most magical city on Earth couldn't find his angel, he was screwed, and not in the battery-powered bunny way.

"Max, you know Helga," he said. "Think. Where would she take her?"

He shrugged. "You know her better than I do, sir. You've always had beef."

"Beef?" He furrowed his brow. What beef could he possibly have with a goose?

"Yes, sir. As I said, she's always been jealous that Eostre chose you."

He groaned and knocked the heel of his hand against his head, trying to jar the memories loose. "That's really what this is about? Jealousy?"

"'An act of hubris is all it takes to bring about the end of days.' That was the third line from the prophecy." Crimson swung the pendulum again. "She sounds like the epitome of excessive pride."

"'Balance dies when birds lie.'" Pete's nostrils flared as he blew out a slow breath. "Helga lied to Eostre. She offered help when she meant to take over the whole operation."

Crimson nodded. "You've forgotten your past. Destiny is awry."

"Oh, dear." Max shrunk inward. "The fifth line."

Pete counted the lines on his fingers as he recited the prophecy Eostre had told to them. "The fifth line is just about Fate willing it. We already knew Fate was playing us like a game of checkers."

Max frowned, his eyes perplexed. "That's the sixth line."

Crimson ticked them off on her fingers. "No, it's definitely the fifth."

Max covered his snoot with his paws. "She didn't tell you all of it."

"Okay." Pete crossed his arms. "Then what's the real fifth line?"

The raccoon shook his head and covered his eyes.

"Max...?" Pete gripped his wrists and gently tugged his paws away from his face. "What's the fifth line?"

His lower jaw trembled. "I can't."

Pete rested his hands on his hips. "You can, and you will. Right now."

"Yes, sir." Max nodded. "Please remember I'm only the messenger."

"We promise not to shoot you," Mike said.

Max drew in a shaky breath. "The fifth line is 'A sacrifice, giving up one life, can stop the war and end our strife.'" He covered his eyes again.

Pete's stomach turned in one direction, his heart in another, until it felt like his innards were swirling in a blender with extra sharp blades. Destiny would not be the sacrifice. The entire fae realm could fall into hell and churn in the tarpits for eternity before he would allow them to take Destiny's life.

"Oh, dear, indeed." Crimson returned to scrying, and Mike's palm glowed red again.

"Don't even think about it," she said.

Mike fisted his hand. "I'm a Devil's Advocate. I can locate her, but you'd have to pay a price."

"Unless you want your furry bunny balls hanging from Satan's rearview mirror, you'll stay as far away from my beloved demon's glowing hand as possible. Trust me." She closed her eyes and whispered another prayer.

"Satan stopped collecting testicles ages ago."

Mike rolled his eyes as if he expected her to know that. "Now he's keeping people's sanity in jars on a bathroom shelf. He's got thousands."

"How big is his bathroom?" Pete asked, taking a step away from the demon.

"Massive," Mike said.

"Oh! I think I'm getting something," Crimson said. "They're in this realm for sure. I... Dammit, I lost it." She opened her eyes. "Looks like it's time for a wild goose chase."

SIXTEEN

"Why are you doing this?" Destiny struggled against the heavy chains securing her wrists. Another set of chains attached the cuff on her ankle to the concrete wall behind her.

"With Pete trapped in the earthly realm, I can finally take what's rightfully mine." Helga waddled toward the person chained to the opposite wall in their makeshift prison. Long, matted hair, the color of dishwater, covered the woman's face as her head hung toward her chest.

"Do you mean Easter?" Destiny twisted her wrists, trying to collapse her hand enough to slide it out of the bind, but the more she struggled, the tighter it got. A painful ache spread from her hands up to her shoulders, her chained leg mimicking the sensation up to her kneecap.

"If so, you didn't have to destroy my bakery. He can't even remember who he is, much less how to cross realms. He's trapped here because of me."

"I know that," Helga snapped. "You did me a favor, and it's the only reason I haven't drained you dry yet. Your time is coming."

The goose honk-laughed. "But this one…"

She used a wing to lift the woman's head. As her hair fell away from her face, Destiny gasped. The goddess of spring, once glowing with youth and vitality, now held an ashy pallor with sunken cheeks, the light in her lavender eyes nearly extinguished.

"Once the realms see what I, the golden goose, can do with Easter, Frigg will have no choice but to make me a goddess. I'll drain this sad excuse for a deity dry, absorb the rest of her power, and take her seat in the hierarchy."

Helga turned Eostre's head from side to side before letting her chin fall against her chest. "I should have been Frigg's choice, not you." She stretched her neck forward and flapped her wings, letting out a honk loud enough to wake every vampire in New Orleans.

"I'm better than you. I always have been." She ruffled her feathers before folding her wings against her body.

So, this was the act of hubris from the prophecy. But Easter was Eostre's holiday, and Pete was the one she'd chosen to carry it out. From what the goddess had told them, even if Helga delivered goose eggs around the world, it wouldn't matter.

"It won't work." Destiny scooted toward the wall, leaning her weary body against it. Her head spun as if she'd been drugged, so she rested it against the concrete. "The fae pantheon will become unbalanced, and even if Frigg makes you a goddess, the seconds it will take for you to fill the seat are all the angels will need to swoop in and claim the realm as their own."

"You don't think I know that?" Helga squawked. "You don't think I've thought it all through? I know what I'm doing better than some defective angel who's been living on a wing and a prayer."

Defective. If that didn't describe Destiny to a T, she didn't know what else could. Coming from a rabid, arrogant goose, the word shouldn't have stung. Helga's opinion of her shouldn't have mattered in the slightest, but "shouldn't" didn't stop it from burrowing into her chest and stabbing her right in the heart.

"She's not defective," Eostre rasped. "She's..." The goddess sucked in a pained breath.

"Save it for the Valkyries." Helga sneered and waddled toward the darkened hall. "Oh, wait. You're dying in prison, not in battle. I'm sure Hel will be happy to hear all about it."

"Where are you going?" Destiny asked.

"To crack the whip on *my elfen*. Someone's got to keep them in line." She honked, ruffled her feathers, and waddled away, humming the tune of "Here Comes Peter Cottontail."

"Are you okay?" Destiny scrambled to her feet, her knees nearly buckling beneath her as she stood. "Why do I feel so drained?"

"It's the iron chains. Fae are allergic to the metal." Eostre lifted her head, leaning it back against the wall. "I'm sure she enchanted them to hold an angel as well."

"But my magic is bound."

The goddess shrugged, wincing with the movement. "I'm afraid she's gotten help from multiple magical beings. I sensed witchcraft in addition to vampirism, and..." Her lids fluttered. It obviously pained her to talk, but Destiny had so many questions, she couldn't help but ask them.

"Is that how she trapped you? With witchcraft?"

"No." Eostre opened her eyes, forcing a sardonic laugh. "She trapped me with trust and my own gullibility. I truly believed she meant to help, to mend our burned bridges. She brought me here under false pretenses and stabbed me with an iron stake. Shock stunned me, and she chained me in my moment of inaction."

"What a bitch." Destiny gasped and covered her mouth, a knee-jerk reaction to the unangelic phrases that had been escaping her lips lately, but honestly...? Who cared at this point? She wouldn't be able to call herself an angel much longer.

Eostre laughed and winced. "What a bitch, indeed."

Destiny pushed from the wall and moved as close to the goddess as her chains would allow before sinking to all fours. "We need to find a way out of here."

Eostre coughed. "Look at me. The longer I'm in the earthly realm, the weaker I become. These chains...and this." She angled her head, exposing the goose-sized bit mark on her neck. "She's absorbing my power. I'm afraid I'm useless."

"No, that's not true. You're a goddess."

"Even the gods can't reign forever. Haven't you heard of Ragnarök? We will be defeated, all the gods killed. It has been foretold."

"But that's just a…"

"Myth?" She scoffed. "Perhaps you've been in the earthly realm too long. The people here so easily dismiss other pantheons as myth when the stories and teachings don't align with their current views."

"You're right, and I'm sorry." Destiny pursed her lips.

"There's no need to apologize. Ragnarök is coming. Your people will defeat us."

"My people? I know angels believe your realm is rightfully theirs and they're ready to take it the second y'all lose balance, but it's giants who are supposed to kill you." At least according to the stories she'd heard.

"That part really is a myth, an alteration of the tale made by earthly beings to relieve their current belief system from blame."

"Well, that…sounds exactly like something people here would do." Destiny sighed, the weight of her drooping shoulders nearly collapsing her. "But it's not going to happen on my watch. Angels and fae aren't so different, you know. I'll figure out a way for us all to get along, but first, you and I have to get out of here."

Destiny sat back on her heels. "I know you're weak, but surely you can still reach out to the ether and send a message."

"I've tried. We're inside an iron mine. My fae magic can't break through." She tilted her head. "But perhaps you..."

Destiny shrugged. "I've been unplugged. I don't have an ounce of angel left unbound."

Eostre lifted her chin, a hint of the regal goddess she was peeking through her pain. "Try."

"I have, back home. I can't even get static."

"Your situation is much more dire. Try again."

She was tempted to tell the goddess it was pointless, but for some strange reason, she felt the need to appease her. Well, okay, the reason wasn't strange. Destiny had always been a people pleaser, but this felt different, like an order she was meant to obey. Whatever enchantment Helga used on the chains was probably making her cuckoo but whatever.

She extended her fingers, pressing her palms together and closing her eyes, trying with all her might to grab a thread of the ether. She might as well have heard *ding, dong, ding, the number you dialed is no longer in service* because she got abso-lutely nothing.

She dropped her hands into her lap. "Blocked. Unplugged. Disconnected. I'm sorry."

"Let's try together." Eostre moved so quickly, Destiny fell backward onto her butt. The goddess reached out, but her chains stopped her from grasping Destiny's hands. "Please."

"Okay, but I don't think any angels are going to come to our aid. They're done with me." She scooted toward her, lying on her stomach and stretching her arms forward. Eostre did the same, both of them lying prone and reaching until their fingers touched.

"We don't need angels. Use what little magic I have left to find Pete. He's looking for you. I'm certain of it."

Destiny's fingers tingled where Eostre touched them. The sensation spread up her hands, the pins and needles reminding her of times when her foot fell asleep. It continued up her arm, lessening in intensity the closer it got to her chest.

The magic wasn't much, but she would use every bit of it to find her fae.

Eostre nodded, and Destiny closed her eyes,

focusing on an image of the man she... Loved? Had she fallen in love with the Easter Bunny?

Why not? Stranger things had happened.

"Focus, my child." Eostre sent a pulse of magic into her. It rolled up her arms and expanded in her chest, making her gasp.

"Pete." She squeezed her eyes shut tightly. "We need you. We're in an iron mine. Please find us."

Her chest heated, creating a series of pops like her heart had turned to bubble wrap and someone was squeezing it. A spark of magic unfurled in the core of her being, but it died as quickly as it had formed.

Frigging Gabriela. She probably had a slew of interns sitting at monitors, wearing their stupid headphones, talking to each other with their stupid little microphones, and watching Destiny's every move. Hopefully that nanosecond flash of magic was enough to alert Pete.

If not...she couldn't even think about the alternative.

"Tell me what you felt," Eostre rasped and folded her arms, resting her chin atop her hands.

Destiny described the popping and unfurling. "But my boss squelched it half a second after it happened. I'm sure she's got the champagne on ice, ready to celebrate my ultimate failure. Ugh."

She rested her chin on her hands, mimicking Eostre's posture. "I feel even worse now."

The goddess's eyes held sympathy. "Iron has that effect on the fae."

"Then remind me not to channel faery magic in an iron mine again." Destiny closed her eyes. Maybe if she took a ten-minute power nap, she could shake the weariness from her body and find a way out on her own.

But her racing mind wouldn't allow it. "What did Helga mean when she said she should have been Frigg's choice? I thought you were the one who chose who would be the Easter Bunny."

Eostre's lips twitched. She pressed them into a line, rolling them inward as if trying to stop herself from speaking.

"I'm sorry. You don't have to tell me." Destiny pushed herself up and sat cross-legged. "Whatever beef you have with the golden vampire goose is your business."

"If you apologize again, I'll clip your wings myself." The goddess winked and sat upright.

"Sorry. Force of habit. I mean..." Her cheeks heated.

Eostre laughed. "The curse of a people pleaser is a hard one to break."

"No kidding."

"You're right. I did choose Pete to be the Easter Bunny." She gingerly touched the bite mark on her neck. "Helga was referring to Frigg's choice for a daughter."

"Choice?"

Eostre nodded. "Frigg had three sons with Odin, while he had many more with other women."

"What is it about gods and infidelity? They think just because they have penises it's okay to whip them out and stick them in any hole they want." Destiny shook her head. "Then again, who I am to judge? My mother wanted nothing to do with me. She abandoned me the day I was born."

Pained sympathy filled Eostre's eyes. "I'm sure she had a reason to—"

"She fell to get away from me. She hated the idea of being my mother so much that she became human as soon as she pushed me out."

Eostre folded her hands in her lap. "Have you tried to find her?"

Destiny scoffed. "No. Why would I? She left my dad to raise me alone, and I..." She pinched the bridge of her nose. "This isn't about me. I'm so—. Please, continue. Frigg wanted a daughter."

"She wanted one desperately, but she couldn't bring herself to try again with Odin."

"Can't say I blame her."

"She is the goddess of motherhood, so she used her magic to turn an *elfen* rabbit into a goddess, into her daughter."

Destiny blinked three times. "You were a rabbit?"

"Indeed, I was, and Helga was furious when I was chosen. Frigg's sacred animal is the goose, so she believed herself the only natural choice. But spring and dawn are soft-spoken and gentle. She needed a daughter with the same demeanor to reign over them, and Helga most definitely was not the one to do it."

Destiny chuckled. "Can you imagine the sun shooting into the sky, skipping the beautiful colors of morning's glory and heading straight to midday like, 'What up, bitches?'"

Eostre giggled. Then she laughed deep from her belly before clutching it. "Oh, it hurts to laugh. But, yes, that is exactly how morning would dawn if Helga were in charge."

"And all the flowers of spring would have razor-blade thorns."

"Indeed. Alas, Helga remains a goose who is never happy with what she has, even with the ability to lay golden eggs. She became livid once again when I chose Pete, an *elfen* robin, to carry out my holiday and ensure I received the proper offerings to continue my existence."

"So you made him a rabbit shifter because the rabbit is your sacred animal?"

"Because I used to be one, yes."

"So, all this. Your life, Pete's life, Ragnarök… Your goose is cooked because an arrogant bird is jealous of you."

"Of me, of Pete, and everyone else who has something she doesn't. She wore an S-shaped neck brace for decades, trying to make herself look like a swan. She is never happy."

"And now she's murdering hens." Destiny crawled to the wall and used it as a brace to stand. Her thigh muscles trembled, and her knees threatened to buckle, but she gathered every ounce of strength she could muster. "Helga has gone too far. I refuse to sit idly by while she destroys your entire world."

And she'd be damned if she'd let a jealous goose

take Pete away from her. With her hands pressed to the concrete, she inched along the wall toward the darkness Helga had disappeared into.

"What's your plan?" Eostre rose to her knees and braced herself against the wall, panting with the exertion. "How can I help?"

"Save your strength. I can't have you dying on me before we get you back to the fae realm." The concrete ended abruptly at a sharp right turn, but the chains stopped her from venturing out of their makeshift prison.

"They fortified this section, which means they probably stored their equipment in here." She turned and finally absorbed the details of their surroundings. Debris littered the floor, and a decrepit shelving unit sagged on the far wall.

She trudged toward it, her brow furrowing, angry determination igniting in her chest, rolling through her veins and energizing her muscles. "Pete's not the only one who knows how to pick locks."

CHAPTER

SEVENTEEN

"Think, Pete. You know Helga." Crimson dumped the contents of her scrying bowl into the sink. "Where would she take Destiny?"

"I don't know!" He flung his arms into the air and paced the length of the kitchen. "I don't know anything anymore. I've forgotten everything."

Without his memories, he was about as useful as a bur stuck to a rabbit's butt. His fated mate was kidnapped, multiple lives were on the line, the end of days was fast approaching, and he couldn't do a damn thing about any of it because he didn't know his head from a hole in the ground.

A hole. Why did—?

"You haven't forgotten; you just can't recall," Crimson said. "There's a difference."

"Is there? Because I sure as hell can't tell." He stopped pacing and tapped his foot.

"Sir, if I may?" Max raised his paw, and Pete nodded. "You're known in our realm for your vivid imagination and your ability to find unique solutions to problems no one else can solve. Perhaps if you focused on the knowledge you have, rather than fretting over the unknown, you could ask yourself the right questions and find your mate."

Aside from the gut-punch reminder that he'd lost his fated mate, that was the most sensible thing he'd heard since...well, since as long as he could remember.

"Where in New Orleans would a day-walking vampire goose with anger issues take an earthbound angel to drain her?" His stomach lurched at the thought, an image of an undead fowl with fangs sucking on Destiny's neck.

"How would that even work?" Mike asked. "Geese don't have lips. How could they cover the wound?"

"Can they even suck?" Crimson asked.

Mike scratched his head. "Maybe if she opens

her mouth all the way, her victim's flesh will mold to the back of her mouth."

"That's how she does it." Crimson raised her index finger. "She deep-throats their necks."

Their banter morphed the intrusive image in Pete's mind into something he could never unsee. He shifted his weight to stop his tapping foot, and a tingle formed in the right side of his brain. It spread over the entire side of his head, wrapping around to the front and flashing a vision behind his eyes.

Destiny sat on a concrete floor, her hands bloodied from struggling against chains. The image vanished as quickly as it had formed, but something else, a feeling...no, a knowing...wriggled into his mind.

He slapped his hand on the counter. "Are there any iron mines in Louisiana?"

Max made a chittering sound and clasped his paw together. "You sense her."

"Barely. She's surrounded by iron ore."

"Why would she take an angel to iron mine?" Crimson grabbed a laptop from a shelf and opened it on the counter. "I didn't think it affected angels like it does fae."

"To keep me from finding her." Pete peered over

her shoulder as she pulled up a map and searched for iron mines.

Mike's phone rang, and he pressed it to his ear before striding down the hall. Max climbed onto the counter, and Crimson gave him a little scratch behind the ears before zooming in on her search results.

"Looks like our choices are Michigan and Minnesota." She pointed to the red pins on the map.

"It's this one. I'm sure of it." Pete tapped the pin on the screen, and it opened a tab with information about the mine. "It's a museum now. She's holding her there, but I can't imagine why she'd do it in a public place."

Crimson lifted one shoulder. "Maybe it's a fail-safe. She knows you can't hop in and out without causing a scene, so she took her to a public place just in case you found her."

He closed his eyes, clearing his mind of everything but the vision he'd seen of his angel. Breathing deeply, he focused on the ether, searching for any information the universe was willing to give up.

It gave him nothing.

"Is the bakery unlocked?" Mike asked as he returned to the kitchen. "Richard is struggling big time. Katrina's got him subdued, but if he doesn't get some cake ASAP, he's going to clear out every grocery store and farm in the parish and cause a real famine."

"There isn't any cake." Pete picked up Max and cradled him to his chest. "Helga destroyed everything."

Mike's eyes widened. "We need those cakes. Only an angel can make them."

"She was planning to contact her boss, but she didn't get the chance." A demon doing demonic things was the least of Pete's worries. "Can you open a portal to the iron mine on the screen? To the concrete room inside where Destiny is. I have to save her."

"I'll call my parents," Crimson said. "The recipe must be recorded somewhere."

"Your parents are angels?" Max asked.

"Long story." She typed on the computer before waving a hand at him. "Send them on their way. I'll handle the cakes."

Mike lifted his arm, his right palm glowing red. "I can get you outside the mine, but you'll have to find the room on your own. When demons try to portal underground, we always end up in Hell."

"That's fine." Pete would find her. All he needed was to get close. Then he'd sense his fated mate.

"Since it's a tourist spot, you might shift before you portal. People won't bat an eye at a rabbit and a raccoon appearing out of nowhere, but a man holding a raccoon is sure to draw attention."

"Right." He set Max on the floor and called on his rabbit. Pastel sparkles gathered around him as his body morphed, his clothes magically absorbing into his animal form.

On all fours, he twitched his nose and looked at Max. "Are you ready for this?"

Max saluted. "I'll follow you anywhere, sir."

Mike sliced a six-inch gash into the fabric of reality and peeked inside, looking right and left before closing it. "There's a wooded area a few hops from the entrance. I'll send you there."

The demon swiped his arm near the floor, creating a glowing red tear in the ether. Pete hopped through without a second thought, and Max scurried in behind him. A rabbit and a raccoon, ready to save the day. Weren't they an unlikely rescue crew?

Then again, they were only going up against a vampire goose. Surely, they could take her down. And if it came down to it, beheading or an iron stake to the heart would take her out completely.

He shuddered at the thought. "I'm a painter, not a fighter."

"Sir?" Max asked.

Pete shook, fluffing his fur. "Nothing. I don't know where that came from." Because he would fight to the death to save his Destiny. He'd take on a gaggle of geese, a scurry of squirrels, and a flamboyance of flamingos...all vampires...all at once, with his paws tied to his tail.

No question about it.

He hopped through a bed of snapdragons that should have been in bloom. Pausing, he twitched his nose, inhaling the scents of earth and arbor, car exhaust, and blacktop. Not a single spring flower was in bloom, not even the local skunk cabbage.

"Poor Eostre," Max said. "All the realms will suffer if you can't save her."

"Surely an *elfen* goose couldn't trap a goddess." He hopped along the edge of the grassy area, the blades just tall enough to hide them.

"Helga is goddess-touched like you, sir." Max crawled behind him. "She can do things no normal *elfen* can, and now that she's a vampire, who knows?"

They made their way alongside the outbuilding without being noticed. A hill emerged from the ground behind it, a locked metal gate blocking the entrance to the mine. Pete crouched low, flattening his ears against his back as a guide led a group of tourists wearing yellow hard hats toward it.

The docent unclipped a keyring from his belt and unlocked the gate, holding it open for the dozen or so people as they stepped inside. He glanced around the area and then pulled the gate closed, locking it behind him.

Pete lifted his ears, turning them this way and that, listening for signs of predators or another group of tourists. "Why can I unlock anything I touch?"

"How else could you sneak into people's back-yards to hide eggs?" Max took a cautious step toward the entrance.

Satisfied with the silence, Pete high-tailed it through the gate and pressed himself against a wall inside the entrance. His heart thumped on over-drive, and he tried to breathe deeply as Max attempted to squeeze through the bars.

His upper torso fit through easily, but his belly stopped him from sliding all the way through. Grab-bing the bars, he pushed with all his might, his jaw clenching and his eyes tightening as he strained. "I shouldn't have eaten so much frosting while I was hiding from Helga. It seems to have gone straight to my hips."

He pushed and wiggled, making zero progress before he slumped between the grates, hanging there like a raccoon-shaped rug on a clothesline. "A little help, please, sir?"

With no humans in sight, Pete shifted, and thank the goddess he really was a fae and not just any old shifter. Fully clothed, he could pretend to be a lost tourist if he got caught. As a buck-naked man...not so much.

"Are you sure it's not the endless supply of chocolate eggs that's the problem?" He offered a hand and used his other to tuck in the belly in question as he pulled.

"Couldn't be." Max laughed, the contraction of his abdomen helping him slip through. He rose onto his back legs and brushed out his fur. "Easter candy honors the goddess. Those calories don't count."

"Good point. Come on. She's this way." Pete trekked through the arched passage, his legs growing heavier and heavier with every step. If he still doubted his faery origins—which he didn't— being inside this mine would've been the definitive proof he needed. Iron was a bitch.

Luckily, it was iron ore surrounding them and

not solid iron. The impurity of ore weakened its effects on the fae, but not nearly enough for Pete's liking.

"You doing okay, buddy?" He paused and turned to Max, whose breathing had become labored.

"I..." He sucked in a breath. "Will follow..."

"Me anywhere. Got it." He kneeled with his back toward his new old friend. "Climb on."

"Thank you, sir." Max clutched his shirt with all four paws, hauling himself up, and they continued deeper into the mine.

Pete's chest tightened and heated, the invisible tether tying him to his fated mate vibrating and pulling, guiding him through the maze of tunnels that branched out in every direction. He made a left and then a right, nearly sliding down a steep slope before it leveled out into a dead end.

No, not a dead end. A narrow tunnel jutted out to the left, and his mate bind yanked him through. He had to crouch, lest his head knock against a wooden beam, and the tunnel grew so dark, he couldn't see his hand in front of his face.

He stepped on something, his ankle rolling, throwing him off balance. His shoulder hit the dirt wall before he could fall, and he kneeled, finding tracks on the ground. With a hand against the wall, he continued, his legs carrying him as fast as the debilitating iron ore would allow. The tunnel made a gradual right turn, and light emanated from a room at the end.

"Des—" He started to call to her. He knew she was there, could feel her waiting for him a few yards away, but he could also sense someone...something...else. Fae magic.

He peeled Max off his back and set him on the ground. "If Helga is in there, I want you to stay back. Understood?"

"Yes, sir." Max lowered his gaze and picked at the fur on his belly.

"You're going to follow me regardless, aren't you?"

The raccoon bared his teeth—his way of smiling. "Anywhere you go."

Pete nodded and crept toward the room, pausing outside the entrance and holding up a hand. Stilling, quieting his breathing, he listened. Two sets of labored breaths. No movement.

"I'm sorry, Pete," Destiny whispered.

At the sound of her voice, he could be cautious no more. He strode into the room, his heart wrenching at the sight of his fated mate, bloodied and bruised, and the goddess, barely breathing, the shine in her aura gone.

Destiny gasped and jerked her head up, her vertebrae cracking as she turned toward him. She squinted, and a single tear rolled down her cheek. "Pete?" she rasped. "Is that really you?"

"In the fluff." He ran to her, dropping to his knees and laying his hands over the chain binding her wrists.

It didn't yield.

He frowned, focusing on the lock and willing it open, but nothing happened. "What the...?"

He grabbed the shackle on her ankle and took a deep breath. "My fae magic always works when I need it, so why...won't...you...budge?"

Destiny grasped his hands. "They're iron. Grab something from the shelf, and we can pick it."

As he rose to his feet, an ear-piercing squawk penetrated the room. He spun toward the doorway, and a flash of feathers and fangs zoomed toward him. Helga opened her bill and clamped onto his nose, rotating her legs like she was riding a bunny-cycle, the razor-sharp claws at the ends of her webbed feet tearing into his neck.

She flapped her wings with vampire speed and strength, throwing him off balance. He careened backward, crashing into the shelf, sending all the contents flying across the room.

"It's mine! *Honk, honk,*" Helga said, her mouth full of his face. "It's all mine."

He grabbed her by the neck and flung her away, but she didn't tumble across the floor like he'd hoped. Instead, her eyes glowed red, and she caught the air with her wings. She flew toward Destiny, wrapping them around her and pressing her fangs against her neck.

"Take one more step and I'll rip out her artery." She tightened her wings around his angel's shoulders. "Bound magic means no healing, means death in seconds." She hissed, and a bit of drool hung from the side of her bill.

"Let her go." He raised his hands, cutting a warning gaze to Max, who quietly crept into the shadows to hide. "She has nothing to do with this."

Helga honk-laughed. "You really are a clueless little rabbit. You can stay in this realm with what's left of your goddess. I'm going to drain your angel dry."

The goose flapped a wing, opening a portal to

the fae realm. Pete kicked a long, thin nail toward Destiny and lunged for her. She grabbed it, but Helga yanked her through the hole, slamming it shut behind them. His outstretched arms met air, and he rolled across the ground, knocking his head against the concrete wall.

CHAPTER

EIGHTEEN

Pete groaned and stumbled to his feet. "Max, can you pick the locks?"

"On it, sir." The raccoon fiddled with the shackle around Eostre's ankle.

"Leave me before the iron drains your magic." The goddess rested a hand on Max's back. "Save Easter. Save my legacy."

"There is no Easter without the goddess of spring, and I'll be damned if that godless goose is going to take your place." Pete grabbed a roll of copper wire and shoved the end into the lock on her wrists. "She's got the woman I love, and no one gets away with hurting my fated mate."

He swirled the wire, and the chains clattered to the floor. Clutching Eostre by the waist, he draped her arm across his shoulders, bracing her weight against him. "Climb up, Max."

The raccoon scrambled up his side and clutched the front of his shirt as Pete rose to his feet. With his dearest friends wrapped in his arms, he stomped three times, opening a rabbit hole in the ground.

"Whoa." That wasn't any old bunny hole. It was a portal to the fae realm. His head spun, but he didn't have time to contemplate what he'd just done. He hopped into the hole, and it closed behind them, opening into his office inside the egg studio.

He lowered Eostre into a chair and stumbled, catching himself on the edge of the desk. The goddess rested her hand on his and lifted her head, the sparkle in her lavender eyes slowly returning. "Do you remember now?"

He gazed at the gilded egg on his desk and picked it up, tracing his finger over the baroque pattern. It was a hen's egg, as all Easter eggs should be. Max climbed onto the windowsill and peered through the blinds into the workshop.

How could he have forgotten his right-hand *elfen*, the most loyal friend he'd ever had? And the goddess who made him into the man he was? The Easter Bunny. Pete Hasen was the one and only Easter Bunny. He had been for over a thousand years, and he would continue to be until the end of days.

"I remember everything." He followed Max's gaze and took in his team of artists, the beloved creatures without whom Easter could not happen. Each *elfen* stood shackled to their workstations, using stencils to paint goose eggs in Helga's image.

He turned to Eostre. "How many days until Easter?"

"Nine."

He nodded. "Then we still have time to save it."

He moved toward the door, but the goddess grasped his hand. "Have you forgotten Destiny?"

"I could *never* forget my fated mate." And he would do whatever it took to wrench her from Helga's clutches.

The goose's unmistakable undead squawk sounded in the studio, and the *elfen* gasped. Pete peeked through the office blinds and found them cowering behind their easels as Helga, her bill full of angel hair, dragged Destiny onto the platform. The iron chains still encircled her wrists, weighing her down, and as Helga forced her to her knees, she groaned.

Pete's nostrils flared, his heart kicking into a sprint.

"Beho—" Helga spit, slapping at her bill until a feather caught the long strand of copper hair tying her tongue. She pulled it out of her mouth and sputtered before spreading her wings wide. "Behold my power, minions. I captured an angel, and I'll drain her dry as an example. Do my bidding, or you'll meet the same fate. I am your master now."

Destiny laughed dryly. "The only thing you've mastered is this idiotic villain monologue."

Helga squawked, ruffling her feathers, and Pete eyed Destiny's hands. She'd gotten the thin nail he'd tossed her into the lock. She just needed to twist it the right way.

"What's the plan, sir?" Max asked, his voice hushed.

Pete glanced at Eostre. Though the faery sparkle had returned to her eyes, her pallor was still ashen, her hair lacking its usual luster. She wouldn't have the strength to end this, so it was up to him to cook that goose.

"Will you be okay alone?" he asked the goddess.

"I am recovering already," she whispered. "Go now. Both of you."

Pete nodded, stomped his foot three times, and hopped into the rabbit hole. Max followed, and they landed at the back of the studio. He took the raccoon's hands in his and sent a burst of Easter magic into his being.

"You've got about ten minutes of my power," he whispered. "Look. The *elfen's* shackles aren't iron. Touch as many as you can and set them free quietly."

"The only reason you could trap me is because my magic is bound," Destiny continued goading the goose. "I'm basically human right now, so big deal. Vampires feed on the mundane every day. Whoop-de-do."

Pete crept toward the platform, crouching so the easels hid him, unlocking the *elfen* he passed along the way. "Stay quiet," he said under his breath.

Helga shook, spreading her wings to take up more space, and three feathers floated to the floor. "There's nothing basic about you, and I am so much more than a vampire."

"If you say so, goose." Destiny stilled her hands, waiting until Helga turned to the crowd to continue working on the iron lock.

"Your precious Peter Cottontail isn't coming to save you. Any of you," Helga honked, and Pete bristled.

That was why he hated that name and the song that went with it. Helga had taunted him with it for centuries, her way of reminding him she believed birds were superior to all other animals.

"I have vampire speed and strength." The goose waved her wings. "I have the power of Voodoo running through my veins and, yes, I even have an angel on my side."

"Why does that not surprise me?" Destiny unlocked her chains, but she held onto them, pretending to still be bound. "I bet her name is Gabriela. Good luck working with her. She'll rake you across the coals the first chance she gets."

"Enough!" Helga lunged and sank her fangs into Destiny's jugular.

Destiny yelped and dropped the chains, gripping Helga's neck with both hands, trying to pry herself free.

Pete shot upright and raced toward them. "Let her go."

"Never!" Helga gurgled, her mouth full of angel blood.

He grabbed her wings, wrenching them behind her body and pulling with all his might. Destiny yanked on her neck, adding to the force and ripping the goose's fangs from her flesh. Blood squirted from Destiny's neck like a fountain. She covered the wound with her hand, but the blood continued to ooze through her fingers. An *elfen* otter fainted at the sight.

Helga lunged and wiggled, trying to free herself from Pete's grasp. He tightened his grip on her wings, wrapping them around her and holding her tightly against his chest. He needed to end this. To end *her*. An iron stake to her heart would do the trick, but he didn't keep the poisonous metal laying around in his studio. That left beheading. But if he chopped off her head in front of his *elfen*, they'd be traumatized for life.

"Honk, honk." In the seconds it took him to contemplate, Helga twisted her long neck around and chomped on his. Her fangs pierced his skin, the searing pain making him lose his grip. She jerked away, taking a chunk of his flesh with her as she flapped her wings and flew to the ceiling.

"I'll be a goddess soon," she squawked. "So I better kill you all while I can."

She dive-bombed the unconscious otter, taking him into her bill and shaking him. Destiny stumbled, the blood loss too much for her to bear. Pete rushed to her, pulling his trusty jar of salve from his magical pocket and smearing the enchanted goo over her wound. The bleeding stopped instantly, and the gash began to heal.

"Are you okay?" He brushed the matted hair from her face.

"I will be." She sat on the edge of the platform, her body swaying as she took a painted goose egg from the nearest box and hurled it at Helga.

The impact made the goose drop the otter, and Max dragged him to safety while the rest of the *elfen* followed Destiny's lead. Helga flapped, rising to the ceiling as goose egg after goose egg soared toward her.

Most of them missed—*elfen* weren't known for their athletic abilities—but a momma possum with her babies on board chunked one right into Helga's face.

The goose fell, thudding on the floor before rising to her feet. "You can't hurt me. I have the healing power of multiple magical beings running through me."

Pete hurled another egg at her head, and she grunted. The *elfen* followed suit, gathering eggs into their arms and chunking them as hard as they could as they encircled her. She tried to fly, but every time she lifted her wings, his beloved team of artists threw more and more eggs.

"Stop!" Helga lowered her head and charged, her webbed feet slapping the ground as she plowed through the crowd. She knocked over three *elfen* before taking to the air and soaring toward Destiny.

"I don't care how many beings you have in your pocket, you're still just a silly goose, and that's all you'll ever be." His angel picked up the iron chain and swung. It crashed into Helga, the force making it wrap around her slender neck two times before Destiny yanked her to the ground.

Stunned silence filled the room as if it had been stuffed with cotton. The pregnant pause expanded, no one speaking, no one moving, everyone barely breathing. Destiny's mouth dropped open, and she covered it with her hand, swaying on her feet as she took in the scene. Pete rushed to her side, steadying her with his hands on her shoulders.

"I didn't mean to do that." Her fingers trembled, and she fisted her hand, lowering it to her side.

"I know." He rubbed her shoulders and followed her gaze to where Helga the golden vampire/Voodoo/goddess-touched goose lay headless on the floor. "But I'm glad you did."

The *elfen* murmured, still clutching their makeshift weapons as they crept toward the body. With the help of the poisonous iron and the strength of one pissed-off angel, Destiny had ripped Helga's head from her neck. Their muttering grew to a chitter, the looks of shock fading from their faces as the energy in the room lightened. A ferret dropped a goose egg onto the floor, stomping on it, and the *elfen* cheered.

Max tipped a box of painted eggs over, spilling them onto the floor. The *elfen* laughed and stomped, singing "Ding Dong the Goose is Dead" as they turned the studio into a giant platter of egg salad.

"They shouldn't be celebrating." Destiny stared straight ahead, her expression blank. "They don't understand what I've done. What's going to happen. This is bad, Pete. So very bad."

The *elfen* gasped in unison, lifting their gazes, and Pete turned to find Eostre standing behind them.

"You know you'll have to clean this up before the hens' eggs arrive, right?" The goddess fought a smile. "Have your fun, my children, and then it's back to work. The hens are already laying."

"I'm sorry," Destiny said, and Pete wrapped his arms around her, pressing his front to her back.

"You ripped it clean off, didn't you?" Eostre said. "That was quite a feat for someone with her magic bound."

"I didn't mean to." Destiny clutched her hands over her heart. "I know what this means. An angel killed a fae. That's grounds to start the war to end all wars. I've single-handedly ushered in Ragnarök, haven't I?"

"No." He held her tighter, pressing a kiss to the side of her head. "Eostre didn't tell you the full prophecy. 'A sacrifice, giving up one life, can stop the war and end our strife.' With Helga out of the picture, the balance will remain intact. You stopped the war."

The goddess's smile faded, and she shook her head. "I'm afraid Helga's life is not the sacrifice the prophecy requires. Take Destiny home. I must meet with the council of gods."

His heart plopped into his stomach to take a swim in the bitter acid. "Eostre, no."

"Take her home, Pete."

CHAPTER

NINETEEN

"It's me, Pete. I'm the sacrifice." Destiny sat in her clawfoot tub, leaning back to look up at him. He'd drawn her a bath and settled her into the tub before showering and changing into the clothes he'd brought from his realm.

His dark hair, still damp, curled onto his forehead, and the intensity in his jewel-green eyes demanded her attention. She wanted to look away, to curl into a ball and drown herself in her own sorrowful humiliation, but he held her gaze, looking, not at her, but *into* her.

His lips moved, beginning to part before he pressed them into a thin line. He took three breaths before he finally spoke. "No one is going to end your life."

Something between a laugh and a sob rolled up from her belly, catching in her throat before coming out on a hard exhale. "It's in the prophecy. Fate has willed it. The angels will turn me over to the fae to stop them from attacking. I might have saved Easter, but I wrote my own death sentence in the process."

Pete stood and grabbed a towel from the rack. "If that's the case, they'll have to get through me first. Come on." He opened the towel, and she stood, stepping out of the tub and letting him wrap her in the soft cotton fabric.

Holding her from behind, he turned her toward the mirror and pressed a kiss to her temple. "You saved us. Eostre will make sure they understand that." He patted her dry before offering the set of clothes she'd gotten from her closet before her bath.

"I suppose it doesn't matter." She dressed in a pair of sunny yellow pants and a white shirt. "You got to the fae realm without a miracle, so my request will be voided. My immortality is already toast, so the best-case scenario would be Eostre convincing your people to let me live out my days as a human. I'll grow old and die, and you'll stay young forever."

She felt like she needed to drink a glass of water, to vomit, and to hibernate for six centuries, but she finished dressing and ran a brush through her hair to make herself presentable. Gabriela would be summoning her any minute now, and she needed to hold her head high no matter what the outcome. She refused to give her boss the satisfaction of seeing her cry.

"You should head back to your realm and help the *elfen* with the eggs. You don't need to witness this."

"Hey, don't say that." He gripped her shoulders before sliding his hands up her neck to hold her face. "We belong together. You are my fated mate, and I will stand by your side until the end of you or the end of days. I love you, and I always will. No matter what."

Her throat thickened, and tears gathered in her eyes. "I love you too, Pete, but... What about when I'm eighty and you still look like you're thirty-five?"

He chuckled and wiped a tear from her cheek. "Then you'll look like the hottest cougar in New Orleans."

She couldn't help but laugh. "You always say the right things, don't you?"

"I try." He pressed his lips to hers, and she closed her eyes, allowing herself a moment to get lost in his embrace.

Everything about this man felt right. The softness of his kisses, the gentle yet purposeful way he touched her, caressing not just her skin, but her soul with each brush of his fingers. His smile made her heart sing, and for the first time in as long as she could remember, she felt like a whole being.

She leaned against him, fitting into his arms as if she were made to be there, and as he deepened the kiss, she knew there was no place in all the realms she'd rather be.

"Gabriela was right." She wrapped her arms around his waist and laid her head on his shoulder. "Any angel who can follow a recipe can do what I do. Crimson's parents proved New Orleans will get along just fine without me."

"It's just a job." He stroked her hair.

"I know that now." She leaned back to look at him. "Maybe in the time I have left, I can learn to just...be."

"Destiny Monroe, you have been summoned."

The voice calling from her living room was unmistakable.

"Gabriela." She closed her eyes for a long blink, preparing herself for whatever news her boss would be all too happy to deliver.

"Are you ready?" Pete offered his hand, and she placed her palm in his.

"Let's get it over with."

They walked hand-in-hand through the bedroom and down the hall toward the living room, both of them stopping short as they took in the crowd standing before them. On one side, Eostre stood, her regal glory fully restored after a few hours outside the iron mine. Next to her stood another goddess with strawberry-blonde hair and a sprinkling of freckles across her nose. With her uncanny resemblance, it could only be Frigg.

A crow perched atop her television, his intelligent eyes taking in the scene. Odin had sent a representative rather than appearing himself. Was that a good thing, or was it a very, very bad sign?

Across from the fae deities stood Gabriela, her chin tipped upward so she could literally look down her nose at Destiny. Michelle stood next to Gabriela, her hands folded at her waist, her expression stoic, and next to her...

"Dad?" Destiny tightened her grip on Pete's hand. "What are you doing here?"

He glanced at the goddesses, his brows knitting as he returned his gaze to hers. "I wanted to be here for moral support when they..." He clamped his mouth shut and lowered his gaze.

Well, that wasn't a good sign.

Pete moved closer to her, the length of his arm pressing against hers as he squeezed her hand.

"Destiny Monroe," the crow said, his voice so deep and ominous, it could only be Odin speaking through him. "You've been summoned by our council for the murder of Helga, my wife's golden goose."

"It was self-defense." Pete moved forward, but Eostre held up a hand. He huffed and stepped back to her side. "Helga was going to kill the *elfen*."

Gabriela sneered. "Destiny is on trial here, not you."

Michelle shot her a cold look, and she closed her mouth, taking a step backward.

Destiny remained silent. She wasn't really on trial, and there was no use in defending herself. She could tell by the looks on their faces this meeting was merely a formality. They'd made their decisions. There would be no negotiations. No pleading for her life. What Fate had willed, no one could undo. Not even the allfather himself.

"Hello?" Jane's voice drifted up from the bakery, followed by several pairs of footsteps on the stairs. "You were supposed to wait until sunset to start this shindig," she said as she strolled into the room.

Gaston entered behind her, and then Crimson and Mike followed, another couple Destiny had never met coming in behind them. Michelle nodded at the couple, her expression as unreadable as ever. She knew them, at the very least, which meant they were probably angels.

"Crimson's parents," Destiny whispered. They had stepped in to replace the cakes Helga had smashed. Gabriela probably called them there to prove a point, to get in one last jab at Destiny's self-esteem before the prophecy was fulfilled.

"I apologize for our tardiness." Gaston bowed at Odin's crow. "My *associate* insisted on changing her shoes before we arrived."

"They're my lucky stilettos. I thought they might come in handy." Jane lifted a foot and winked at Destiny.

Michelle cleared her throat. "Destiny, as I am sure you are well aware, our pantheons have been at odds for millennia. Our truce has held for centuries, both sides keeping to our own realms to maintain peace."

"That's not true. You don't all stay in your own realms." Jane raised her hand, and Destiny tried not to cringe. "Plenty of fae call New Orleans home, and Destiny has lived here for a long time too."

"Because this realm is considered neutral ground," Destiny said through clenched teeth, giving her head a warning shake. Her friend was only trying to help, but talking back to an angel of Michelle's caliber always ended badly.

"You're lucky we've already smited your kind." Gabriela crossed her arms.

"I think you mean smote." Jane mimicked her posture.

Crimson whispered something into Jane's ear, and she rolled her eyes, dropping her arms to her sides before making a face at Gabriela.

"I tire of this banter," Odin said through his crow. "Destiny, as a citizen of the angelic realm, you murdered a fae, thus ending the truce. Angels, this is your chance to make amends. What is your offering?"

Michelle opened her mouth to speak, but Gabriela beat her to it. "We offer you her life. We'll strip her wings and halo permanently, rendering her human. You can do with her whatever you like."

Gabriela smirked at Destiny and swiped her hands across each other as if finally ridding herself of the burden.

"Your offering is accepted," Odin said. "We will take her life, and the truce will remain intact. Frigg, Eostre, see to it." The crow flapped its wings twice and disappeared in a cloud of black glitter.

Frigg gestured at Destiny, and Michelle strode toward her.

"I'm so sorry, honey," her dad said as he hung his head. "I tried to keep you safe."

"You can't do this." Pete shoved her behind his back, spreading his arms as if he could actually stop it from happening.

"It's okay." She tugged on his arm, but he refused to move. "You can't get in the way of angelic business unless you want to be on trial too."

"They can string me up by the fluff on my nuts before I'll let them hurt you." He jerked his head toward the goddesses. "Eostre, Destiny saved Easter. She saved *us*. Surely you didn't agree to a death sentence."

"Step aside, Peter," Eostre said. "All her people will do is strip her angelic magic."

"I won't let this happen." His eyes were wild, his pulse sprinting in his veins as Destiny clutched his wrist and stepped around his outstretched arms. "Don't."

"It's okay." She faced Michelle and let him go. "I'm ready to accept my punishment."

Michelle's expression didn't change. Not even an ounce of pity or sympathy creased her brow as she laid a hand on Destiny's chest.

Her stomach tightened, a heavy ball forming in her gut before drifting upward and expanding in her chest. Pinpricks gathered on her skin beneath Michelle's palm, and the ball vibrated, rattling her to the core of her being. The room seemed to spin around her, and her head felt as if it might literally explode.

The sensation dissipated, and Michelle stepped away. "It is done."

Destiny swayed on her feet, but as the room stilled, she didn't feel pain or emptiness like she expected. She simply felt lighter.

Michelle returned to Gabriela's side. "Her life is yours. Do with it what you will."

"No!" Pete grabbed Destiny's arm and stomped the floor, no doubt to open a rabbit hole and whisk her away.

"Not now, Peter." Eostre held a hand toward him, and he froze. "Behave yourself, or I'll send you home before we finish with her."

Gabriela snickered. "I can't wait to see this."

Michelle cut her another look before turning to the goddesses. "What other charges have you brought against us?"

Other charges? Destiny rubbed her chest and leaned into Pete. "If it's about his amnesia, I take full responsibility. Please don't let my mistake affect the truce between our realms."

"That is noble of you to say." Eostre smiled softly.

Frigg glanced at her before turning her attention to Gaston. "Vampire, what evidence did your council uncover?"

Gaston straightened and stepped forward. "*Madame, Mademoiselle.* We discovered the vampire responsible for turning your golden goose and punished him accordingly."

"With a stake in the heart." Jane made a stabbing motion before mouthing *it's more fun with my boot* at Destiny and wiggling her ankle.

"Ahem." Gaston glared at Jane before continuing. "Before the culprit expired, our interrogators were able to glean information about Helga's endgame. She wished to usurp, not Eostre, but Odin himself."

"And how did she plan to do this?" Frigg asked.

"You are aware of how she devised to insert herself into your council." Gaston clasped his hands behind his back. "Once there, she intended to invite a team of angels to attack, giving them whatever insider information she could gather. She colluded with one angel in particular, who agreed to split the fae realm, allowing Helga to rule one part while she reigned over the other."

"Which angel in particular?" Eostre arched a brow.

"That one." Jane pointed at Gabriela. "Now can I use my lucky boots?"

"That will not be necessary," Michelle said.

Gabriela scoffed. "Can you believe this? Me colluding with a vampire duck? The absurdity of it makes me laugh."

Michelle rolled her eyes and pressed her palms together. "Gabriela, you are sentenced to five hundred years in the repository, after which our council with the fae will reconvene to determine if the punishment has sufficed."

"What?" Gabriela shrieked. "You can't be serious. You believe them?" She flung her arm at the vampires before glaring at Destiny. "You believe that sniveling little runt over me, your star manager?"

"Star ass kisser is more like it." Destiny crossed her arms, apologizing for her language not even crossing her mind.

"You're broken." Gabriella jabbed a finger at her. "You always have been."

"I'm not broken." Destiny raised her head, straightening her spine. "I'm fine just the way I am, and I'm sorry I ever let you make me feel otherwise. You're the one who's broken."

Gabriela gasped and narrowed her eyes, her jaw ticking before she opened her mouth. "You—"

Michelle flicked her wrist, sending her to the repository in a cloud of baby blue dust. Then, she leveled her gaze at Destiny. "This will be the last time I see or hear from you. I will leave you to your punishment. Mark, return to our realm as soon as it has been dealt."

"Yes, ma'am," her dad said, and Michelle disappeared into the ether.

"Now, Destiny." Frigg laced her fingers together. "About your life."

CHAPTER

TWENTY

Destiny's head spun, and nausea churned in her stomach. This was it. Her thread of life was about to be snipped, and a pair of fae goddesses wielded the scissors.

"Eostre, I did what I could," her dad said, his brow knitting. "You have to do something. Help her, please."

"What needs to be done will be, Mark. Have you lost all faith in me?" She gave him an odd look and shook her head.

Destiny cut her gaze between them. Normally, she'd ask them why they were speaking to each other like they were old friends, but that was the least of her worries at the moment.

"What the fluff is going on?" Pete squeezed her hand. "Whatever you're planning to do, you'll have to go through me first. You can forget about Easter, and you'll be right back to square one. I don't care about balance. All I care about is her."

"Calm down, Peter." Frigg chided him. "You'll change your tune in a moment, but first, Destiny, my dear. You worry about your demon friends and the balance you were meant to keep in New Orleans."

"I..." What could she say? Yes, she worried, but it was out of her hands now.

"My mom and dad are going to take over," Crimson said. "They're moving back to New Orleans for good."

"Well..." Her chest ached, and she leaned into Pete, letting him support her weight and the gravity of everything happening. At least her friends would be taken care of, and Crimson would get to see her parents more.

"We just wanted to say hello," Crimson's mom said. "Your recipe is perfect, and we'll take good care of it."

"Take care of my bakery too," she forced the words over the lump in her throat.

"Oh, we'll be working out of our coffee shop in

the Quarter. We'll leave y'all to it." She waved and led her husband downstairs.

"We will be going as well." Gaston gestured to the exit.

"The hell we will," Jane said. "Destiny is my friend. I'm not leaving her now, in her time of need."

"Come, *ma chère*. This is not our affair." He clutched her arm.

"But—"

"Jar it." He dragged her toward the door.

"You mean *can it*," Jane said, fighting his pull.

"It's okay." Destiny gave her a tiny wave before hugging Pete tighter. "It's best if you all leave for this."

"Are you sure?" Crimson asked.

Destiny nodded. Her friends didn't need to witness what was about to happen. "Yeah. Go on."

"Okay. Take care." Crimson took Mike's hand, and they followed the others out the door.

"You can't take her." Pete held Destiny to his chest, turning her away from the goddesses. "I love her. She is... She's everything, and I don't want to live a single day without her. I don't care if she's human. I don't care if she's a vampire/zombie/hellhound demon. I love her, and I need her. She's my Destiny. She's mine."

"Come here, child." Eostre reached for her, but she hesitated.

"No." If Pete held her any tighter, she'd pop.

"Peter," Eostre spoke in a motherly tone that said *you had better cool your jets or I'm going to knock you into next week.*

Destiny reached a shaky hand toward the goddess and peeled herself out of Pete's embrace. "I love him too. I know it's wrong, it's forbidden, or...it used to be forbidden when I was still an angel, but..."

Eostre held both her hands, her irises sparkling like lavender glitter. "It's not wrong, and thanks to you, it will no longer be forbidden."

"I don't understand."

"Tell her, bunny," her dad said. "It's time she knows the truth."

"Bunny?" She glanced at Pete, who raked a hand through his hair, looking as perplexed as she felt.

"I lied to you," her dad said. "Your mother didn't fall. She couldn't because she wasn't...she *isn't*...an angel."

"I still don't understand." Destiny furrowed her brow as she tried to comprehend what he was saying. Her mother wasn't an angel? Angels and humans got together all the time. There would've been no reason to lie about it. Unless her mom wasn't human.

The pieces began to fall into place, and she sucked in a sharp breath. "You?"

Eostre nodded, a tear sliding down her cheek. "Your father and I fell in love at a volatile time. The truce had just been stabilized, and our realms had agreed to a hands-off policy. We couldn't let anyone know about our relationship or our child, so we concocted the story. Your father raised you because our people would have killed you if they discovered you, the daughter of a goddess, were half-angel."

Destiny tugged from Eostre's grasp, crossing and uncrossing her arms as she processed her words. *The daughter of a goddess?*

"Leaving you was the hardest thing I've ever done." Another tear slid her cheek. "But it was the only way to protect you."

She shook her head. It didn't make sense. "Angels and fae can't have children. Our DNA isn't compatible. It's not possible."

"It is when you're a descendant of the goddess of motherhood." Frigg smiled, her pale blue eyes twinkling.

"It is indeed." Eostre laid a hand on Destiny's abdomen.

"Wait. Am I...?" Her stomach looped, all the blood in her head plummeting to her feet. "With Pete?"

"Destiny." He rushed to her, taking her in his arms and lifting her from the ground. "We really can multiply like rabbits."

He set her down and took her face in his hands. "I love you so much."

"I love you too." She blinked rapidly, the tears hanging out on her lower lids refusing to fall. "So the fae aren't going to kill me because I'm..." She rested a hand on her belly.

"You're one of us, dear," Eostre said. "Even if you weren't pregnant, you are still a fae."

"The sacrifice from my prophecy was your angelic life." Frigg touched her shoulder. "You gave up one life, hopefully to embrace another. It was never our intention to murder you."

"You could have led with that." Destiny pressed a hand to her chest and sank onto the sofa. "So all this time...all my flubs and imperfections were because I wasn't one hundred percent angel?"

"Your definition of perfection is an illusion." Pete sat next to her, resting a hand on her knee. "You've always been perfect to me."

She laced her fingers through his and gazed up

at the goddesses...her fluffing mom and grandma! "But if I'm half-fae, why don't I have any fae powers? I'd kill for a set of Pete's magic pockets."

"Wouldn't we all?" Eostre laughed. "I had to bind your fae magic when you were born, but your daughter has awakened it. Your immortality remains intact, and your powers will continue to grow inside you as your baby does. Why else do you think Helga's iron chains made you feel sick?"

"She enchanted them. You said..."

"I lied." Eostre waved a hand. "She'd have killed you instantly if she knew you carried Pete's child."

Destiny nodded. "Another thing for her to be jealous of."

"Indeed," Eostre said. "We will give you two a moment, and then, Pete, you must join the *elfen* in the Easter preparations. They need you."

"Can I help?" Destiny squeezed Pete's hand.

"You are always welcome in our realm," Frigg said. "Mark, when Easter is over, you and Eostre must devise a plan to inform your higher ups. From this moment forward, the fae are no longer forbidden from having relationships with angels."

"I look forward to it." He smiled and winked at Eostre before turning to Destiny. "I'm sure you have a few bones to pick with me. Whenever you're ready to talk, just let me know."

Destiny swallowed the thickness from her throat, thankful he didn't ask her to process all her emotions at once. "I will."

He nodded, and, in a cloud of silver sparkles, he returned to the angelic realm.

"We'll see you both soon." Eostre smiled softly, and both goddesses disappeared into the ether.

Pete grasped Destiny's other hand, angling his body toward her. "How are you feeling?"

She gazed into his eyes and chewed the inside of her cheek as she allowed the emotions to wash through her. There were so many, she couldn't begin to name them all. "Stunned. Relieved, I guess. Overwhelmed is probably the best word right now."

"It's a lot to take in." He tucked her hair behind her ear. "How do you feel about us? About her?" He rested a hand on her stomach.

Her muscles contracted beneath his touch. "I feel a bit like Romeo and Juliet, minus the death by poison. Carrying a baby Easter Bunny and uniting two realms was not on my bingo card today."

He chuckled, holding her gaze until she answered his question.

"I'm yours forever, Pete, and as for her..." She laid her hand on his. "I'm over the moon."

"She's definitely the icing on the cake."

"What about you?" she asked. "How do you feel about everything?"

"I'm elated. I get to spend eternity with the woman I love and raise a child together." He brushed his fingers across her cheek. "And I remember everything, who I am, where I came from. Right now, in this moment with you, I truly have it all."

So did she, it seemed. "What made you remember?"

"You did." He pressed his lips to her forehead. "When Helga took you, the only thing in the world that mattered to me was getting you back. My fae magic works when I need it, right?"

"I guess it does."

"I needed to get to the fae realm—to you—more than I'd ever needed anything in my life. The second I hopped down the rabbit hole, it all came rushing back."

"You're you again," she said.

He smiled. "I'm me, but I'm not the same guy I was before. I'm whole now, thanks to you."

Warmth spread through her chest. Her angelic

life might be over, but she'd choose Pete over centuries of miracle requests any chance she got. "For the first time in my existence, I feel whole too. Thanks to you."

"We're more than whole." He rubbed her stomach. "We're multiplying."

"And it's electrifying." She laughed and rose to her feet, tugging him up with her. "Come on. We better go save Easter. No miracles required."

"Not as long as I've got you." He grinned and stomped his foot three times, opening a rabbit hole in the floor. "Let's bounce."

Also by Carrie Pulkinen

Fire Witches of Salem Series

Chaos and Ash

Commanding Chaos

Claiming Chaos

Mayhem and Ember

Mending Mayhem

Mastering Mayhem

Collection One: Books 1-3

Collection Two: Books 4-6

New Orleans Nocturnes Series

License to Bite

Shift Happens

Life's a Witch

Santa Got Run Over by a Vampire

Finders Reapers

Swipe Right to Bite

Batshift Crazy

Holy Shift

Collection One: Books 1-3

Collection Two: Books 4-7

Crescent City Wolf Pack Series

Werewolves Only

Beneath a Blue Moon

Bound by Blood

A Deal with Death

A Song to Remember

Shifting Fate

Collection One: Books 1-3

Collection Two: Books 4-6

Haunted Ever After Series

Love at First Haunt

Second Chance Spirit

Third Time's a Ghost

Love and Ghosts

Love and Omens

Love and Curses

Collection One: Books 1 - 3

Collection Two: Books 4 - 6

Stand Alone Books

Flipping the Bird

Sign Steal Deliver

Azrael

Lilith

The Rest of Forever

Soul Catchers

Bewitching the Vampire

ABOUT THE AUTHOR

Carrie Pulkinen is a paranormal romance author who has always been fascinated with things that go bump in the night. Of course, when you grow up next door to a cemetery, the dead (and the undead) are hard to ignore. Pair that with her passion for writing and her love of a good happily-ever-after, and becoming a paranormal romance author seems like the only logical career choice.

Before she decided to turn her love of the written word into a career, Carrie spent the first part of her professional life as a high school journalism and yearbook teacher. She loves good chocolate and bad puns, and in her free time, she likes to read, drink wine, and travel with her family.

Connect with Carrie online:
CarriePulkinen.com